DANGEROUS STRANGER

by

LUCY GILLEN

HARLEQUIN BOOKS

TORONTO
WINNIPEG

Original hard cover edition published in 1972
by Mills & Boon Limited, 17-19 Foley Street,
London W1A 1DR, England

© Lucy Gillen 1972

SBN 373-01683-2

Harlequin edition published May, 1973

Printed in Canada

1683

OTHER

Harlequin Romances

by LUCY GILLEN

Many of these titles are available at your local bookseller,
or through the Harlequin Reader Service.

For a free catalogue listing all available Harlequin Romances,
send your name and address to:

HARLEQUIN READER SERVICE,
M.P.O. Box 707, Niagara Falls, N.Y. 14302
Canadian address: Stratford, Ontario, Canada.

or use order coupon at back of book.

CHAPTER ONE

MELODIE got up from her chair by the window as quietly as possible, trying not to wake her grandfather. She tiptoed across the room and looked down at the pale, wrinkled face that looked so much older that it should have done. Sometimes when she saw him as he was now her heart was moved to almost unbearable pity, for only a few years ago James Neil had been a giant of a man—a grandfather whom she had adored all her life and whom she was prepared to nurse for the remainder of his.

She bent instinctively and kissed the top of his head where thinning grey hair showed the white scalp through. The thin hands folded over the blanket that covered him stirred at the touch and the eyelids flicked upwards to reveal surprisingly bright, dark eyes in the drawn face.

'I'm sorry, Grampy,' Melody apologised. 'I didn't want to wake you.'

The old man smiled. 'Like the Sleeping Beauty,' he told her with a flash of his irrepressible humour, 'I wake to a kiss.' He looked out at the bright sunshine and shook his head at her. 'You shouldn't be indoors on a day like this,' he told her, 'you should be out in the sun.'

'Wouldn't you like me to sit with you?' she asked, and again he shook his head.

'I'd much rather you were out in the fresh air, I'm perfectly all right, lass.'

'I was thinking of going for a walk,' Melody confessed, 'but I don't like leaving you, Grampy.'

A mischievous smile animated the sunken features and for a moment Melodie was reminded of the grandfather she had once known. Traces of the strong, handsome features still remained and were revealed sometimes when he smiled and teased her, like now, and the dark eyes looked bright and shiny despite the lines that pain and tiredness had drawn round them.

'Don't you trust me alone with Mrs. Bazeley?' he asked, a dry laugh crackling in his throat at the idea of their plump and eminently respectable housekeeper being in jeopardy.

'You wicked old rogue,' Melodie told him, 'I wouldn't trust you with anyone else.'

James Neil chuckled delightedly, reaching for her hand. 'You go for your walk, lass, I'll be all right in Mrs. Bazeley's care. I shan't run away,' he added with poignant solemnity.

'I'll only be about half an hour,' Melodie told him, 'and then we'll have tea when I come back. O.K.?'

'Are you seeing Jed?' he asked, and Melodie nodded.

'I expect so, he's usually there about now.'

'Then don't hurry back on my account, love,' her grandfather told her.

The old man knew she met Jed Martin most days, although they seldom spoke of it, and she carefully refrained from letting him know just how serious Jed had become lately because she knew he would encourage her to see Jed more often and never give a thought to his welfare, something she was not prepared to do, even for Jed.

'I shan't hurry,' she assured him, 'but I can't keep

you waiting for your tea, can I? And Jed understands.'

The old man regarded her for a moment thoughtfully, and Melodie thought she knew what he would say next. It was a question that had risen many times before and she was always just as vehement in her denials.

'It's not much of a life for you here, Melodie, is it?' he asked. 'Not after working in that big hospital with hundreds of other people, you must get lonely for it.'

She shook her head, as she had done so many times before during the same argument. 'Now don't start that again, Grampy,' she scolded him. 'You know I love being here, and I've told you so a hundred times before.'

'So you have,' the old man agreed with spirit, 'but that doesn't mean to say I have to believe you. You see so few people and go out so seldom, it isn't right at your age.'

'It is if I'm happy here,' Melodie insisted, 'and I am. Now stop fussing, Grampy.'

It was not a very strenuous life, although it was limited for social opportunities, but she only spoke the truth when she said she was happy at Millway. She had always loved staying there when she was a child and afterwards when she had time off from the hospital. It was almost a year ago now that the doctors had informed his family that the old man would never get any better and would require constant nursing, although he was not completely bedridden, and it had seemed the most natural thing in the world for Melodie to give up her hospital job and take care of him. She had always loved Grandfather Neil and it had been no hardship to come and live at Millway.

Then there was Jed. Jed Martin owned the land that

7

adjoined her grandfather's to the east and she had met him first when she was walking back from the village not long after she arrived, and he had almost knocked her down with his car as she crossed the road.

Despite his rather reticent manner it had been fairly obvious from the start that he had been captivated, as others had been before, by the small, heart-shaped face with the riot of copper-red hair and green eyes, and he had wanted to see her again. Since then they had met fairly often, sometimes by arrangement, mostly not.

Jed was a widower, she had learned, living with his small son and his mother in the rambling old farm-house they had moved into after Jed's wife died. Reading between the lines and judging by the one brief meeting she had had with her, Melodie guessed that Mrs. Martin senior was a quite formidable matriarch and ruled the household with a will of iron.

She based her judgment, she freely admitted, on guesswork and assumption, for Jed had never once made complaint about his mother or her ways. He adored his son, she knew, and wanted him to be other than a farmer, but the boy's grandmother was from farming stock for generations back and she firmly discouraged any other ideas. The boy himself seemed, at the moment, unconcerned about anything beyond running in the fields and riding the pony Jed had bought him for his birthday.

Melodie loved the country and it had been no hardship for her to exchange her previous rather hectic existence for the quiet life at Millway. The old man looked at her, smiling understanding, but shaking his head. 'I should have a conscience about keeping you here,' he told here, 'but I believe you are happy here in a way.'

'In every way,' Melodie assured him. 'Now, is there anything you'd like me to get for you before I go out?'

'Nothing, thank you.' He shook his head. 'Remember me to Jed.'

'I will,' she promised, although in fact the two men had never met. She was very doubtful if they would get on together if they ever did meet, for in his prime James Neil had been a forthright, outspoken man who feared nothing and no one, a rather aggressively flamboyant man with a unquenchable sense of humour, while Jed was much more serious and quiet. Quiet sometimes to the point of being self-effacing, it seemed to Melodie, although he had enough stubborn native Yorkshire grit to know what he wanted and go after it in his own way.

Melodie breathed deeply as she left the house, relishing the warm, spicy smells of late summer that the recent rain had enhanced rather than diminished—the smell of hay almost ready for cutting and of meadowsweet and clover warmed by the sun.

There was little of her grandfather's once prosperous farm left to him now, for encroaching ill-health had forced him to sell off most of it to someone better able to farm it, and where his fields had stretched out to the acres away to her left, there now remained only the one narrow strip that was bounded by Jed's land on one side and Keith Scott's on the other, swallowed up by the neighbouring farm and uncropped except where Keith Scott's sheep strayed on to it.

Thinking of Keith Scott, Melodie pulled a wry face and her usually soft mouth tightened involuntarily. When she had first come to Millway to live, nearly a year ago, the neighbouring land had been farmed by old Mr. Crowe, but three months ago the old man had

9

died and the executors had sold the farm, lock, stock and barrel, to a newcomer and, worse, not even a Yorkshireman. It was rumoured that he was not even an Englishman, but some kind of a foreigner, although Melodie had some doubts about that, since his name was British enough even if his appearance wasn't.

Their first encounter had not been a happy one for Melodie, and none of their encounters since could be called exactly friendly. They had some kind of argument each time they met it seemed and always Melodie got the worst of the encounter although she was invariably in the right.

It had all started when she had been obliged to tell him that he had no business riding across Millway land, and several times since she had had cause to complain about his sheep straying. True, the hedges on his side were her grandfather's responsibility, but she had other things to think about than having hedges repaired.

What was worse, he had actually had the temerity to complain, in retaliation, that the ditch on the Millway side was dangerous to his stock when they got through the hedge, and he had suggested, in no uncertain terms, that the repairs to the hedge should have been done long ago.

Neither old Mr. Crowe, who had originally bought the land from her grandfather, nor her grandfather had ever kept livestock in that field and therefore the question of straying had never arisen. Keith Scott, on the other hand, used it to graze sheep, and Melodie attributed the action as much to his stubborn refusal to change his mind as to any other reason and she had said so more than once. Let him put the field under hay, as it had always been, he had acres of good pasture

10

elsewhere.

She pulled a wry face and admitted, but only to herself, that most of the rancour in the exchanges was on her side, for he seemed to find the whole thing rather amusing—a reaction which neither pacified her nor endeared him to her.

She walked at her usual steady pace, enjoying the warmth of the sun and the soft swish of the uncropped grass under her sandalled feet. The distant, undulating shimmer of the moors lay hazily sprawled as far as the horizon under a sky almost unbelievably blue, with the hills rising smooth and rounded in the distance off to the west, and the silver cross-stitch of streams meandering their casual way across the valleys.

The low hedges surrounding the farmland did little to distort the view and on both sides of her the creamy-white dots of sheep straggled over the landscape. Beyond the hedge on Keith Scott's side, where the farmland bulged out into the moor, a wide deep lake glittered in the sun like molten silver where the light breeze rippled across its surface. The loss of the lake had been one of the hardest things to bear as far as Melodie had been concerned, for it held such happy memories for her.

She started towards the spinney where she invariably saw Jed, and then suddenly changed direction when she saw something that attracted her attention. A man was standing on the Millway side of the hedge, apparently busy at something, and that alone was enough to make her curious. He was so engrossed in his task that he did not even notice her approach at first, but raised a red and rather startled face when she called to him.

'What are you doing there?'

He waited until she came nearer before he answered and she recognised him as one of the men from the village who often did odd jobs of hedging and ditching, as well as anything else that needed attention and for which regular labour was not readily available.

He gave her a half-wary smile and nodded his head as she came nearer. 'Afternoon, Miss Neil.'

'Hello, Mr. Bardsley.' She looked at the work he was doing, at the neatly layered hedge and the pile of cuttings. 'Oh, I see you're repairing the hedge.'

'Aye.' The man pushed his cap to the back of his head with a thumb, and looked a bit sheepish. 'It's wrong time t'year, a course,' he told her, 'but it needed doin', Miss Neil.'

'I suppose it did,' Melodie allowed, her suspicions already aroused as to who had ordered it done, 'but we didn't ask you to do it, Mr. Bardsley.'

'Nay, I know.' He scratched a searching thumbnail over his stubbly scalp and looked apologetic enough to confirm her suspicions. 'Mr. Scott asked me if I'd do it, yon sheep keep getting through.'

Melodie faced the inevitable with a resigned sigh. 'I see—well, you'd better finish it now, and I'll see Mr. Scott about it later. In the meantime see my grandfather for your pay, Mr. Bardsley; it's our hedge, after all.'

'Well—I dunno.' He looked further discomfited and the thumbnail was busy again in his grey thatch. 'Mr. Scott already paid me in advance, miss.'

'He paid you?'

'That's right.' He looked at her, rather slyly, she thought, and with a glint of amusement in his small sharp eyes. 'Mr. Scott,' he confided, 'reckoned you might spot me workin' here and he didn't want you to get no wrong ideas, miss.'

Melodie flushed at the very idea of the man making an accomplice of George Bardsley. It did not take too much imagination on her part to picture the two men giving each other sly looks as comment on the vagaries of women in general and herself in particular.

'I don't think I *have* got any wrong ideas,' she informed him shortly. 'This hedge is my grandfather's responsibility and his property and he's quite capable of paying for its repair and maintenance.'

'Aye well, I don't know about that, I just know I bin paid for't job already.'

Melodie looked at him for a moment, reminding herself that it was not George Bardsley's fault if Keith Scott was an arrogant and overbearing creature who took things into his own hands just as it suited him. She smiled understandingly. 'I'm not blaming you for anything, Mr. Bardsley,' she told him. 'And you're very honest,' she added. 'You could quite easily have kept quiet about having been paid for the job already and been paid again.'

The red, weathered face showed surprise at the suggestion and he shook his head. 'There's nowt t'be gained from them sorta doings, Miss Neil. Folk talk, an' if I were found t'be a sharp'n, I'd not get t'work.'

'No, no, of course you wouldn't.' She looked at the neatly repaired hedge approvingly. 'You do a very good job.'

'A man can do nowt more'n his best,' he told her.

'Well, I'll see Mr. Scott and settle up with him,' she said. 'If you see——'

She glanced up then, attracted, as he was, by the soft, drumming sound of hooves on the soft ground and the glimpse she had of his expression before he bent

13

to his task again, she would have sworn there was a knowing smile on his face. 'He'll like as not tell you himself,' he informed her, and Melodie watched the approach of her least favourite neighbour with a glint of anticipation already shining in her eyes.

Whatever else she could fault in Keith Scott, she had to admit that he rode a horse better than anyone she'd ever seen, even though he did it with the same arrogant air he brought to everything else.

He was taller than most, well over six feet, she guessed, and as dark as night. It was darkness that owed a great deal to the outdoor life he led, but she was convinced that there was something else responsible for it too. His skin was tanned to a deep, golden brown that went well with jet black hair but looked strangely at variance with the deep blue of his eyes. Had it not been for them and the very British sound of his name, Melodie would have had no difficulty in believing the rumours that he came from some other country, and one with a much warmer climate.

He sat the big black he rode, easily as always, appearing relaxed and casual although the spirited animal must have taken quite a bit of holding. His mount too was not the type of animal one expected to see a Yorkshire farmer riding, at least not as a working horse, and yet she had seldom seen him on any other, except occasionally an equally well-bred but rather bad-tempered grey mare.

Somehow the sight of the two of them, so perfectly in harmony, never failed to stir something in her that she could never quite explain. There was a sense of power and strength that emanated not only from the powerful black but from the man who rode him as well.

14

He reined in the horse and smiled across the hedge at her, sparing a brief glance for George Bardsley so engrossed in his task. 'Hello, Melodie.' He had used her christian name for some time now, informing her, with his usual arrogance, that three months was plenty long enough to remain on formal terms with a neighbour, especially when they enjoyed such good arguments as they did, a statement she did not agree with.

'Good afternoon, Mr. Scott.' Her own views had not coincided with his and she still, stubbornly she admitted, used his surname and a very formal 'Mr'.

The deep blue eyes looked across at her for a moment before he swung himself down from the saddle. He could quite easily have got over the hedge, for there was no ditch on his side and plenty of room to step down on the other, but he was apparently intent on being polite about it this time. He raised an enquiring brow at her. 'Shall I come over to your side or will you come over to mine?' he asked.

Melodie had to admit to a sudden desire to giggle at the solemnity of the question and the very polite tone, but she was aware of George Bardsley's interest, however well he might be trying to hide it, and she shook her head.

'Is it strictly necessary to do either?' she countered, and he laughed.

His laugh was something she always found oddly disturbing and she felt her fingers curl into her palms at the sound of it. 'I want to talk to you,' he informed her, 'and I'm *sure* you want to talk to me, and the width of the hedge, not to mention the ditch, is rather cramping my style. Also,' he added, glancing at George Bardsley with a meaningful smile, 'while I know George wouldn't mind hearing us wrangle over the job he's doing, we're not going to oblige, so——you choose. Your side or mine?'

Melodie glanced at her watch. 'I'm not sure I have time to talk to you at the moment,' she told him, and he laughed again, this time making it sound as if he was not fooled for one minute by her ruse.

'I don't think Jed Martin will mind being kept waiting for a few minutes,' he told her softly, his eyes glittering with satisfaction at having struck a sensitive spot.

'How do——' she began, and he shook his head. He must have seen her with Jed, of course, it would be easy enough with no more than half an acre across to the spinney, and they never made any secret of their meetings. Nevertheless it gave her an oddly vulnerable feeling to think that he had seen them and perhaps found their way of meeting rather amusing.

'I've seen you,' he told her, and Melodie glanced uneasily at George Bardsley.

'You'd better come down to the gate,' she told Keith Scott, 'I want to see you about paying for the hedge repairs.'

She disliked the smile of satisfaction he gave her at having won his point, but decided to ignore it. 'I'll give you a head start,' he said, 'as you're on foot.'

She nodded briefly and set off along the edge of the meadow towards the small stream that bounded her grandfather's property and divided it from the open moor before curving outwards to encompass the wider land which now belonged to Keith Scott. The little stream shone and bubbled in the sun and provided a pleasant destination on summer days.

She glanced across towards the dim shade of the spinney, but there was, as yet, no sign of Jed. It was disturbing to know that their meetings had been observed and noted and she must remember to tell Jed that they must meet somewhere less conspicuous; perhaps further into the trees. Not that they had any reason to hide, but the idea of Keith Scott seeing them and probably finding the idea amusing was not to her liking at all.

A moment or two before she arrived at the five-barred gate that divided the two properties, Keith Scott flashed by on the other side of the hedge and by the time she arrived he had tethered the black to one of the posts and was perched on the topmost bar of the gate, waiting for her. He looked as if he had been there for ages and glanced very pointedly at his wristwatch as he got down from his perch.

'Do you always keep men waiting?' he asked.

'Not from habit,' Melodie retorted, 'but you could hardly expect me to keep pace with that great creature.'

He smiled and shook his head over her disparaging reference to his mount. 'That great creature, as you call him,' he informed her, 'is a pure-bred aristocrat, you should treat him with the deference due to him.'

'He *is* beautiful,' Melodie allowed, 'and much too good to be used as a working horse.'

He laughed softly, the sound trickling along her spine as she met his eyes. 'He earns his keep like the rest of us,' he told her, 'but I agree he's very beautiful and like most beautiful creatures he needs a great deal of very careful handling or he runs amok.'

The implication was obvious, but she chose to ignore it. 'We're not here to discuss the merits of your mount,' she reminded him coolly, 'but the fact that you've seen fit to employ someone to do repairs on our property without consulting my grandfather first.'

17

'Would I have been allowed to?'

Melodie blinked, a small frown drawing at her brows. 'Allowed to?'

'Consult your grandfather?'

'Well, no, not personally, he's a very sick man, but you could have consulted me on his behalf.'

'For the thousandth time,' he retorted, 'that hedge was like that when I took over from old Mr. Crowe, and I've told you about getting it repaired over and over again.'

Melodie stuck out her chin. 'Perhaps if you'd *asked* me instead of telling me you'd have been more successful,' she told him, and he looked at her with raised brows.

'I doubt it! Do you mean to tell me,' he added after a quizzical study of her face, 'that that's the only reason you've done nothing about it? Because you didn't like the way I spoke to you about it?'

'In a way,' she admitted. 'That was one reason.'

'And the other?'

She kicked at a tuft of grass, unwillingly honest. 'I—I forgot.'

He stared at her for a moment, then burst into laughter while Melodie stood beside him feeling very small and gauche and wondering what on earth had possessed her to be so honest about it. 'You forgot!' He looked at her steadily, the deep blue eyes alight with laughter, shaking his head slowly. 'Well, at least you're honest enough to admit it, but how do you expect me to keep my sheep in their own pasture and out of your wretched ditch when you forget to get the hedge repaired? I can't stop them getting through and then there's hell to play.'

'I merely objected to your sheep wandering all over

our land,' Melodie objected, feeling a bit self-righteous now that she had confessed to the truth. 'That's not playing hell.'

'You weren't on the receiving end of it!' he retorted. 'And just how *was* I supposed to keep them in with the hedge as it was?'

'You could have grazed them somewhere else,' she said. 'Grampy never put livestock in there, neither did Mr. Crowe.'

'Well, I do,' he told her, in a voice that brooked no argument, 'and it's my property now.' He eyed her speculatively for a moment, leaning back against the gate, his brown face curious. 'That's partly what rankles with you, isn't it, Melodie?' he asked.

'Nothing rankles with me——' she began, but she might not have spoken for all the notice he took.

'The fact that I've now got what was once your property?'

She was silent for a moment, a rather startled look in her green eyes as she wondered how much truth there was in what he said. There was little enough left of what had once been a large and prosperous farm, but there was no one of the old man's sons who took an interest in farming, and Melodie was the only one who shared his love of the country. She had spent so many happy years there that she supposed she did, in some ways, resent anyone else taking it over.

Perhaps most of all she regretted losing that deep, cool lake where she had so often sat and dabbled her feet in the water, and which was now out of bounds to her. Yes, she had to admit, that perhaps she *did* resent him being there, although she had not minded when old Mr. Crowe had it.

'That's—that's silly,' she said slowly at last, and so

doubtfully that he recognised it at once and shook his head.

'Not so silly,' he denied, 'and in a way it's understandable, although I don't quite see why you should have developed a passionate hatred of me just because I bought the place.'

'I haven't—I mean, I don't hate you,' Melodie said, and saw his brows lift in comment, though she found it difficult to interpret just what it was she saw in his eyes.

'I'm very relieved to hear it,' he told her, 'but you're not exactly enamoured of me either, are you, Melodie?'

'No.'

He laughed then, teasing her unmercifully. 'That I presume,' he said, 'is what is known as Yorkshire bluntness?'

'You asked me,' Melodie declared, 'so I told you.'

The deep blue eyes regarded her for a minute in thoughtful silence and she knew her cheeks were warm with colour. 'You really do dislike me, don't you?' he said at last, and his surprise seemed genuine. Also he was not, for once, laughing at her, indeed he looked at her steadily and quite solemnly as if he found it hard to believe. 'Why?' he asked when she did not answer. 'Apart from the fact that I bought the farm from old Crowe, what else have you against me?'

'I——' She sought for words and found none that were the complete truth. Her feelings towards him were too far complex for her to either recognise or explain, and he grinned at her suddenly and knowingly, as if he saw her predicament and enjoyed it.

'There you are,' he declared, full of self-confidence, 'nothing! Nothing but what your stubborn and unreasonable little feminine mind makes you imagine.'

'I'm not unreasonable,' Melodie denied, stung to self-defence. 'I'm just trying not to be rude.'

'Well, don't let me stop you,' he said. 'Go ahead, be as bluntly Yorkshire as you like.'

She stuck her nose in the air, determinedly polite. 'Definitely not, I don't know you well enough to be—to be so outspoken.'

He looked at her steadily for a moment and in a way that set her heart hammering nervously against her ribs. 'That,' he said quietly, 'can soon be remedied.' He shortened the distance between them to inches and one large hand covered her throat, the fingers gripping her chin while he swept her against him with his free arm and brought his mouth down over hers in a kiss that drove the breath from her.

She struggled wildly when she at last realised what was happening, and pushed her hands against him. 'You——' Her green eyes blazed furiously at him, although her anger was as much for her own initial compliance as for him, and he seemed not in the least disturbed by it. 'Of all the conceited, arrogant, insufferable——!'

'That'll do to be going on with,' he told her, and to her chagrin, he laughed.

'How dare you laugh at me!'

His face sobered but left his eyes still bright with laughter and he released her with seeming reluctance. 'Whew!' he declared, wiping the back of one hand across his forehead. 'Jed Martin must have his hands full with you, my girl. I'll bet he trembles in his shoes every time you frown.'

'Jed!' She put a hand to her mouth, her eyes wide, anger momentarily forgotten when she remembered Jed. If Keith Scott could see her with Jed, it stood to

21

reason that, out here in the open by the gate, Jed could quite easily see them, and she turned with more haste than care, forgetting in her haste the end of the ditch where the ground dropped suddenly away.

'Look out!' He made a fruitless grab at her as she fell and the ground seemed to fall from under her feet without warning. Fortunately there was plenty of long, coarse grass at the edge and she grabbed at it as she felt herself going, clinging on desperately to prevent herself from toppling into the stagnant water only inches from her face.

'Get me out!'

She heard a deep chuckle from just above her and a moment later she was hauled with more strength than gentleness back on to the bank. 'Whoops-a-daisy!' He had big strong hands and they made light work of lifting her, still retaining their hold even after she stood, rather shakily, on her feet.

She blinked at him uncertainly for a moment, bewildered by the suddenness of it, then she pushed herself free and began brushing grass seeds and pollen from her frock while he watched her.

She had seldom felt so embarrassed in her life, firstly because of the way he had kissed her, and secondly because she had been so befuddled by it that she had fallen in the ditch like a complete idiot and given him the chance to laugh at her again. 'Thank you,' she said, refusing to look at him.

'What for?'

'Pulling me out of the ditch, of course.' She looked up then and met his eyes, her soft mouth tightening when she saw the laughter there. 'I'm glad you find it amusing,' she told him.

'Well, you did look rather comical, with your feet

22

in the air and hanging on to a tuft of grass for dear life,' he told her. 'But if I'd known how ungracious you were going to be about it, I wouldn't have bothered.'

'I'm surprised you did!'

He looked at her silently for a moment. 'Oh no, Melodie,' he said softly. 'You're not really, are you?'

She knew he was right, she wasn't really surprised but she hesitated to admit it, then finally shook her head. 'No,' she said at last. 'But you could have been more gentle and—and sympathetic about it, instead of laughing.' He made no reply, but after a moment his hands reached out for her and it was only by sheer good luck that she didn't fall into the ditch again when she backed away from him. 'What—what are you——'

'I'm just going to show you how sympathetic I am,' he told her, with a wicked gleam in his eyes. 'And gentle too, believe it or not.'

'I—I believe you.' She looked at him wide-eyed and wary, disturbed by the wild racing of a pulse at her temple and the way her knees felt weak and trembly.

'Don't you want me to prove it?' She shook her head firmly and he shrugged. 'I'm disappointed, especially since Jed Martin's over in the spinney.'

'Oh no!' She turned, more carefully this time, then hastily looked back when she saw Jed's familiar brown head and stocky figure at the edge of the spinney.

Although she had backed away from him, he was still much too close for comfort, and she wished he would not look as if he found the whole thing such a huge joke. 'Waiting patiently,' he told her, 'like Jacob for Rachel.'

'Nothing of the sort,' Melodie denied hastily. 'But I must go, I'm late as it is.'

'What about the business we started to discuss before we got sidetracked?' he asked, as if he sought to keep her longer, and she shook her head.

'My grandfather will pay for the work that's been done,' she told him. 'Please let us know how much you paid George Bardsley and we'll settle with you.'

'Is that your grandfather's decision or yours?' he asked quietly.

Melodie frowned. 'I know Grampy will want to pay you, Mr. Scott, so please take my word for it.'

The brown face crinkled into a smile again and he pushed his hands into the pockets of his riding-breeches, his blue eyes taunting her. 'I'll take your word for it,' he promised, 'but I'll come over and see your grandfather tomorrow, just the same.'

'No!' She was uncertain just what made her so adamant about it, but she had a strange feeling that the old man might actually like Keith Scott and she was unwilling to put her suspicion to the test. He raised an expressive brow and she sought for reasons to put him off. 'He's a very sick man,' she told him. 'He doesn't see anyone.'

'No one at all?'

'Well—only very few people. Only those he knows well, excitement isn't good for him.'

'Then he must have a pretty hectic time with you,' he suggested, and Melodie frowned.

'I happen to be a qualified nurse, Mr. Scott, and I know what's good for my patient.'

That, she realised, took him by surprise and he looked at her curiously for a moment. 'Are you really?' he said at last. 'I didn't realise that.'

'I don't suppose you did,' she said. 'Now I really must go, Jed's waiting for me.'

'Melodie.' A hand on her arm stayed her further.

'Are you quite certain it would be dangerous for me to come and see him?' he asked, and she found herself unable to meet his eyes when she answered him.

'Not dangerous,' she admitted. 'But I—I'd rather you didn't, Mr. Scott.'

'Why?' The hand still rested on her arm and she was forced at last to meet the deep blue eyes which held her gaze steadily, so that she could neither look away nor lie to him.

'I—I don't exactly know,' she confessed, and heard him laugh softly.

'Then I'll be there.'

She lifted her chin, ready to argue, then thought better of it and instead turned and walked away, rather stiffly and self-consciously because she knew he was watching her. Across the meadow to the spinney where Jed still waited for her. One of these days, she thought, she *would* get the better of Mr. Keith Scott.

CHAPTER TWO

ALL next morning Melodie was on tenterhooks, wondering if Keith Scott really would come over and see her grandfather as he had threatened. She had given the old man only an edited version of what had happened, carefully omitting any mention of the way she had been kissed, or her ignominious fall into the ditch. She had waited until the next morning to tell him anything at all, and then only because she feared the consequences if Keith Scott should visit the old man.

Her grandfather was confined to a chair in the house,

but he still took an interest in what went on around him, and particularly anything to do with Millway. He would not take kindly to being kept in ignorance about his neighbour's rather high-handed action if he had learned of it from the man himself.

He raised a brow over the information that George Bardsley had already been paid for repairing the hedge and the tired brown eyes glistened when she related the ensuing argument, much abbreviated, and she thought he was as angry as she had been herself, until a dry chuckle betrayed amusement rather than anger and she saw her hopes of support in that direction coming to nothing.

'He's no Yorkshireman,' the old man decreed, 'chucking his brass about like that.'

'He's a bit of a mystery to everybody,' Melodie told him. 'He's definitely not local and I can't guess where he comes from—I just know I don't like him.'

That wasn't strictly true, she recognised a moment later, but it was said now and the old man was looking at her with curious eyes. 'Oh? Why not, lass?'

'I don't really know,' she was forced to admit at last. 'Except that he's arrogant, opinionated and—and conceited and——'

The old man chuckled delightedly. 'He sounds quite a man,' he told her, the shrewd old eyes watching her closely. 'He's certainly discovered your sensitive spot, lass, hasn't he?' The frail hands folded down the edge of the blanket carefully, and he watched her face as he spoke. 'What's he like, this feller? To look at, I mean?'

Melodie plumped cushions, determinedly casual and unwilling to commit herself on that point. 'I—I suppose he's passable,' she allowed with a shrug. 'Tall, very dark, in fact he'd pass for an Italian or a——a

26

Spaniard if it wasn't for his eyes.'

'His eyes? What's wrong with his eyes?'

'They're blue; deep, dark blue, and he has ridiculously long lashes for a man.' She pulled herself up sharply, aware of her grandfather's sly smile and the warmth of colour in her cheeks. 'I suppose,' she added casually, 'a lot of women would find him attractive, although he's not at all good-looking.'

'But you don't, eh, lass?'

Melodie looked startled. 'Me? I haven't even thought about it, Grampy, I was much too busy feeling guilty about keeping poor Jed waiting.'

'I wonder he didn't come over and see what you were about,' her grandfather declared bluntly. 'Seeing his lass with another man; I'd have been over there sharpish when I was a young man.'

'Maybe you would, Grampy,' she told him with a laugh, 'but I'm not sure Jed looks on me in quite such a possessive way, or even if I'm his lass, as you term it. Anyway,' she added, as much for her own satisfaction as his, 'he'd know I was doing no more than discuss business or something with Keith Scott.'

'Then he's not got much get up and go,' the old man retorted. 'A pretty lass like you, he should make up his mind one way or t'other whether he's coming or going. What's he taking so long for?'

'Grampy, Jed and I are good friends, no more.' She tucked the blanket in around him more firmly and refused to look at him. 'Also he knows better than to be jealous of Keith Scott.'

'Didn't he even ask what you'd been talking about?' he demanded. 'I would have done in his place, even if we were only—only good friends. Only good friends,' he repeated scornfully, 'what sort of a phrase is that?'

27

'A true one,' Melodie insisted. 'He didn't ask because he didn't have to. I told him we were talking business and he took my word for it.'

'Aye,' the old man declared, '*my* business. I hope young Scott does come over, Melodie,' he added. 'I've a fancy to meet that young feller.'

'I especially asked him not to,' Melodie said. 'You shouldn't have visitors, not strangers anyway, and especially Keith Scott.'

'Nonsense! He's not likely to launch a physical attack on me, is he?'

'No, of course not,' she said, 'but I just don't think you should have a visitor who's likely to start some sort of—of controversy about the hedges, that's all. You'll only get over-excited and then you'll be poorly again.'

'Stuff!' the old man retorted with surprising vigour. 'I *like* talking to folks, and I'm curious about young Scott.'

'He's not all that young,' Melodie told him, seeing her arguments demolished. 'He's in his middle thirties, I should say.'

The old man chuckled wickedly. 'That may be old to you, lass, but to me he's still a lad.'

'Not old,' Melodie objected, 'I didn't——'

'But old enough to make you mind your manners,' the old man interrupted, thoroughly enjoying himself at her expense—a trait, she only now realised, he shared with Keith Scott.

She got on with her dusting. 'Anyway,' she told him with a certain satisfaction, 'it doesn't look as if he's coming. It's lunch-time now, and he's the type who'd come charging in before anyone had time to clean and tidy the place.'

'Ready to impress him?' he asked slyly, and Melodie

28

flushed.

'Nothing of the sort,' she denied. 'But no one likes being caught before the normal household chores are done.'

'Well, if he comes and I'm dozing,' he said, 'you wake me, girl. You hear?'

Melodie sighed, acknowledging the inevitable. 'All right, Grampy, if that's what you want, but please try not to get too excited.'

The old man chuckled wickedly, his dark eyes more bright than she had seen them for some time. 'I'll leave that to you, lass,' he told her.

Melodie was unutterably relieved that by the time she set off to meet Jed that afternoon, the threatened visit had still not materialised. Perhaps, she thought hopefully, he had forgotten all about it, or else he had had second thoughts. Even Keith Scott was probably guided by his conscience sometimes.

As she crossed the meadow, she automatically looked across to where George Bardsley had been working yesterday, but there was no sign of anyone today, only the tidy evidence of his labours, and she had to admit to a great improvement. Keith Scott's sheep were safely confined to their own pasture now and could no longer stray on to Millway land.

She arrived at the edge of the spinney just ahead of Jed, turning to smile when she heard him coming. There was something so reassuringly ordinary about Jed, which she found welcome after her encounters with Keith Scott.

He took her hand and brushed his lips lightly against her forehead. 'Melly!' Jed was the only person who ever called her Melly and she had never yet dared mention as much to her grandfather, for it had been he who chose her name, and he would have hated to hear it so distorted or in any way abbreviated. He smiled, pleased to see her, as always, although he made no great show of it. 'I'm sorry I'm a bit later than usual,' he told her, 'but I got held up.'

'Oh, don't worry,' Melodie said, as they strolled along just inside the edge of the trees. 'I've only just come.'

'How's your grandfather?' He never failed to ask after the old man, although he had never met him.

Melodie smiled, remembering the spirited repartee she had exchanged with the old man just before she came out. 'Verbally at least he's in great form,' she told him. 'Although in fact, of course, he'll never be any better. Sometimes he's so—so bright and mischievous it's difficult to believe he's so ill.'

'It's hard on the old man,' Jed agreed, 'but you're a wonderful girl to give up your whole life to him the way you do, Melly. He's very lucky to have you.'

His rather sad-looking hazel eyes looked at her earnestly and she smiled. He was slightly less than six feet tall and rather heavily built. He would probably become very stout later in life but at the moment he looked reassuringly sturdy and solid. His thick, light brown hair was cut very short and made his round, homely face perhaps look bigger than it really was. He rarely smiled and never laughed, but Melodie found him kind, understanding and dependable.

'I'm lucky to have a grandfather like him,' she told him with a smile. 'He's a wonderful man, Jed, and he never complains. He just sits in his chair all day and——' She shook her head over the future. 'I can't believe he has so little time left,' she said softly. 'He was always so full of life. He laughed a lot, drank far too much at times, but he was so wonderfully alive and alert, and now he—I could cry when I think of him, Jed.'

'Don't do that, love, it'll not do either him or you any good.' A comforting arm encircled her shoulders, hugging her close, and she knew there was far more compassion there than the words might convey. 'You've done your best for him and—well, when his time comes you'll have earned a bit of happiness of your own.'

Melodie shook her head. 'I can't bear to think of him not being here,' she said.

'Maybe not, lass.' The encircling arm tightened momentarily. 'I've thought of it lately,' he confessed, 'but it's different for me, I know. I want to get wed again, and you know how I feel.'

'Jed——'

'Oh, I'll not rush you,' he went on without giving her time to finish. 'You've to do right by the old man first.'

Nothing, she thought, would ever make Jed into an impatient lover and she wondered, briefly, why the knowledge gave her a twinge of impatience. Romance was not Jed's big point and she could not help regretting it sometimes. The rather stark unromantic announcement that he wanted to marry again was, she supposed, by way of being a proposal and she could do nothing about the disloyal thought that flitted through her mind, that Keith Scott would have made the occasion a more memorable one.

'There's so little I can do for him,' she said. 'I try to keep him quiet, as far as I can, but he's such a—a mischievous old love. He delights in visitors and

31

they're really not good for him.'

'I've been thinking I should come over and meet him,' Jed told her. 'I suppose with your parents living away, he's your nearest family, isn't he?'

'Yes, but——'

'There's plenty of time, of course,' he added hastily.

'Oh, but I'm sure he'd love to meet you,' Melodie told him, feeling rather as if she was forcing the issue when he seemed so reticent. 'You'd be welcome to come over any time, you know that, Jed.'

He frowned a bit over that—Jed was nothing if not cautious. 'It'd be best to set a time,' he decided. 'I don't like just dropping in on folk unexpected like.'

'Oh no, of course not. Well, suppose I speak to Grampy first, and see when suits him best, how's that?'

Jed nodded, apparently well satisfied that the niceties were being observed. 'Good,' he said. 'Then let me know.'

'I breathed a sigh of relief when I came out just now,' she confessed. 'Because Keith Scott hadn't come over as he threatened.'

'Threatened?' He took her literally of course, and stared at her in surprise. 'Good lord, you don't mean he——'

'Oh, of course not,' she amended hastily. 'It wasn't a threat, he simply said he'd be calling to see Grampy about George Bardsley doing the hedge and I thought he meant it, but he hadn't come by the time I left, so I gather he had second thoughts.'

'But didn't you say he'd paid Bardsley for the job?'

'Yes, that's the whole point,' she explained. 'It's our hedge and we're quite capable of paying to have it repaired.'

'Maybe your grandfather'll not be so quick to agree

with you on that,' Jed remarked with sound Yorkshire logic. 'After all, it's for Scott's benefit that the hedge needed repairing and he's plenty of brass to play around with, from what I hear.'

Melodie looked at him curiously. 'What *do* you hear, Jed? He's a complete enigma as far as I can see. Even his looks puzzle me.'

'He doesn't look English,' Jed agreed, cautiously, 'but that doesn't mean to say he isn't and he's spent a lot of time abroad.'

'It could be,' Melodie allowed, trying to put her finger on just what it was that made her doubtful. 'But there's something about him somehow.'

'Well, you've seen him more often and closer to than I have,' Jed remarked, 'so I'll take your word for it.'

It was hardly possible, she thought, that she had really detected a hint of reproach in his voice, as if he was jealous of the fact, and she remembered uneasily the way Keith Scott had kissed her yesterday. Surely if Jed had seen that he would have spoken of it when she saw him only shortly afterwards.

'I see him far more often than I like,' she informed him. 'Mr. Keith Scott isn't my cup of tea at all.'

'Has he been bothering you?' he asked, and for a second Melodie looked at him uncertainly.

'Why—why, no,' she said. 'Except with those wretched sheep straying, of course, and now the hedge has been repaired that won't happen again.'

'I just wondered.' He walked along in silence for a few seconds, looking down at the ground, obviously searching for words that were not easy to come by. 'It was when I saw you over there yesterday,' he went on after a while. 'You seemed annoyed about something and he was laughing. It seemed a bit odd, but'—he shrugged—'you seemed to be coping, so I didn't want to poke my nose in.'

Would he have behaved differently, she wondered, if he had arrived a few minutes earlier and witnessed the way Keith Scott had kissed her and the way she had allowed herself to be kissed until common sense made her protest as she should have done in the beginning?

She remembered her grandfather's rather tart remarks about Jed's lack of action and wished she could have proved him wrong. It was very doubtful, she thought wryly, if Jed was jealous or saw any reason to be.

'It was the inevitable argument,' she told him. 'We're always arguing—he's that sort of neighbour.'

'Maybe I should have a quiet word with him,' Jed suggested very unexpectedly. 'Tell him to mind his p's and q's when he's dealing with you. Put right a thing or two.'

Like telling him he intended marrying her, Melodie thought, and shook her head with a faint smile. 'Oh, I don't think that's necessary, Jed,' she told him. 'It's all too petty to make a big issue out of it.'

'Aye, that's as maybe,' Jed declared, apparently warming to the idea of a confrontation with Keith Scott, 'but he looks the sort who'd go chucking his weight about with women. It'd do no harm to have a quiet word.'

'I'd rather you didn't,' Melodie insisted. 'Please Jed.'

'All right,' he agreed, but there was still a stubborn look about his mouth, as if he would like to have pursued the matter. 'But if he starts getting out of line,

Melly, let me know. He's bit of a mystery, and I don't like mysteries.'

Melodie smiled. 'There've been enough rumours about him at various times,' she said, 'but no one really seems to *know* anything, it's most intriguing.'

'He has letters with a foreign postmark,' Jed declared with authority, and Melodie blinked.

'Oh?'

He nodded, as if quite sure of his facts. 'Mrs. Clark thinks it's Argentina. She thought it was Africa at first,' he explained, straight-faced, 'but then she decided it was Argentina.'

'But how on earth does Mrs. Clark know so much about——' She nodded at last, and smiled understanding. 'Ah yes, of course, Mrs. Clark works at Crowe's farm part-time, doesn't she? Sort of on–off cook housekeeper.'

'That's right,' Jed agreed, 'and Mrs. Clark's Mrs. Gowk's sister.'

Mrs. Gowk was his daily woman, and obligingly garrulous on village gossip. The surprising thing was how, with her sister working for Keith Scott, the man still managed to remain such a mystery. 'I'd forgotten for the minute,' she said. 'I suppose Mrs. Gowk passed it on to you?'

'To Mother, actually,' Jed said, precise as usual. 'She also said,' he added casually, 'that Mrs. Clark's had instructions to get two more rooms ready for next week—he's having visitors, apparently.'

'Oh?' Melodie's curiosity was well and truly aroused now and she made no secret of it. 'Now who can that be, I wonder?'

'You sound interested,' Jed told her, and sounded a bit put out at the idea.

'Well, I am, I suppose,' she admitted. 'I was wondering if they were male or female, and if they're any relation to him.'

'Why?'

She shrugged. 'Oh, nothing really, I was just remembering the old adage, that's all—that the female of the species is more deadly than the male.'

It was something of a shock when Melodie got back to learn that they had a visitor. She returned to the house via the back door and the kitchen, and Mrs. Bazeley looked up from her potato-peeling to raise a brow. 'There's company,' she informed Melodie, with customary abruptness.

'Company?' For the moment she had forgotten Keith Scott's promise, and she stared at the woman with startled eyes.

'T'feller from Crowe's,' Mrs. Bazeley enlarged. 'He said Mr. Neil was expecting him, so I showed him straight in.'

'Keith Scott! I might have known!' She frowned as she hurried across the kitchen, followed by Mrs. Bazeley's slightly surprised gaze.

'I didn't do owt wrong, did I?' she asked before the door was open, and Melodie shook her head hastily.

'No, Mrs. Bazeley, it's all right, you weren't to know.'

'He seems a decent enough young feller,' Mrs. Bazeley declared, 'an' your granddad seemed right pleased to see him.'

'Yes. Yes, it's all right, thank you.'

Melodie hastily crossed the hall, uncertain why it was that her heart was hammering away so heavily at her ribs. She could hear voices coming from the sitting-

36

room at the front of the house. The deep, quiet one she recognised as unmistakably Keith Scott's, with her grandfather's less strong but making itself heard for all that. The laugh was definitely her grandfather's and he seemed to be enjoying himself immensely.

She opened the sitting-room door and the visitor immediately got to his feet, looking even more incredibly tall in the confines of the room. He was a little more formally dressed too, in a well cut tweed jacket and grey trousers, although he still wore a sweater-type shirt and no tie.

The deep blue eyes swept over her briefly in a way that made her flush with more than the anger that already sparkled in her eyes for the way he had waited for her to go out before he came. 'Hello, Melodie.'

The familiar greeting, she could see, did nothing to offend her grandfather's sense of propriety, in fact there was a definite gleam of mischief in his eyes when he looked at her. 'I've got company, lass,' he informed her perkily. 'This feller came after all, you see.'

'I do see,' she said. 'After I specifically asked him not to.'

'Aye, he was smart enough to wait until you were out of the way before he came,' the old man told her cheerfully.

'Just as I might have expected Mr. Scott to do,' she retorted. 'You should be resting, Grampy.'

'Oh, stop fussing, for heaven's sake, girl,' her grandfather told her shortly. 'I'm right as rain. It'll do me no harm to have a good laugh for a change. I was never a man for sitting around waiting to die of boredom.'

'Grampy!'

It had never really occurred to her before that the once lively old man might be unutterably bored with

37

nothing to do all day and the reminder shocked her. Worse was the sudden look of pity that showed in Keith Scott's eyes. It told her not to worry, that the old man did not mean what he said, and the idea of his being so understanding made her feel worse.

'Oh, it's not your fault, lass,' the old man said, as if he too had just realised the effect of his words. 'I'd be better if I was a reading man, but all my interests only ever required energy, not brains.'

Melodie smiled, won over as always by the sheer charm of her patient. 'I'll teach you to knit,' she threatened, 'and see if that will keep you out of mischief.'

'People's what I like,' her grandfather told her. 'Like Mr. Scott here, somebody I can talk to and have a laugh with.'

Melodie looked at the visitor, then hastily lowered her gaze before the expression she saw in his eyes, her pulse fluttering uneasily. How much had he told her grandfather, she wondered, and what had they been finding so amusing when she came in? It was conceited, of course, to suppose that they had even mentioned her at all, but just the same she could not help but be suspicious.

'I've told you many times, Grampy, that visitors aren't good for you,' she said. 'I told Mr. Scott too, but he chose to ignore my advice.'

'Good job,' the old man declared, 'I've enjoyed myself better than I have for months. He's going to stay and have tea with me too,' he added determinedly. 'No matter how much you fuss and fume, my lass.'

'Oh, not if Melodie really objects to my staying,' Keith Scott protested, so meekly that Melodie looked at him and frowned.

'This is my grandfather's house, Mr. Scott,' she told him, deliberately discouraging. 'He's issued the invitation.'

'But you're all for evicting me right now?'

'I didn't say that.'

'Then please, Melodie, may I stay and have tea?'

She knew that if she looked either at him or the old man she must, inevitably, burst into laughter. There was an expression so amazingly similar in the two pairs of eyes that watched her that she retained her self-control only with difficulty.

'I'll go and tell Mrs. Bazeley we'll be one extra for tea,' she said, and crossed the room to the door, maintaining as much of her dignity as possible, closing the door behind her with a disapproving bang, just to let them know she was not won over.

Mrs. Bazeley said little when Melodie told her, merely commenting that the parkin would never last out the week at this rate. She raised no other objection, and in view of her apparent approval of the visitor earlier, Melodie began to feel rather like the odd man out.

She pushed the tea trolley into the sitting-room a few minutes later and seated herself behind it, doing her best not to appear over-enthusiastic and very conscious of those deep blue eyes fixed on her with speculative amusement.

'You look prissy, girl,' her grandfather informed her. 'Don't look so disapproving.'

'I didn't know I was,' Melodie said, and the old man shook his head.

'Showing off,' he declared knowingly, and winked at Keith Scott in a way that made Melodie flush with embarrassment.

39

'Grampy——' She shook her head over the pointlessness of arguing with him. It was no use protesting to her grandfather that she was no longer a little girl to be reprimanded in front of visitors. Instead she picked up the plate of parkin and offered it to Keith Scott.

He took a piece, murmuring his thanks, and a moment later raised an expressive brow. 'Very good,' he remarked.

The old man smiled delightedly. 'The best in the county,' he informed him.

'I believe it.' Keith munched appreciatively. 'I must get your Mrs. Bazeley to show my Mrs. Clark how to make parkin like this. Hers isn't bad, but this is delicious.'

The old man chuckled, watching Melodie's pink-flushed face with wicked eyes. 'You'd better get Melodie to show her,' he said. 'She made that.'

'Really?' The surprise, she thought, was rather overdone, as if he thought her incapable of doing anything as praiseworthy as baking a good parkin. 'You *are* well gifted, aren't you?'

'Am I?' She felt much more embarrassed than she should have done, and wished her grandfather had not been so ready to boast of her achievements.

'But of course.' The blue eyes were watching her, she knew, but she refused to look at him. 'You're a nurse, which is quite an achievement in itself, and now I find you're an excellent cook as well. Then to crown it all you're—beautiful.' The last word was spoken so softly and in such a way that she felt her fingers curl into her palms the way they did when he laughed. He was really the most disconcerting man and he seemed to care little that her grandfather was there.

She flicked him a hasty glance from under her lashes and was rather surprised to see him apparently serious. 'I—I like cooking,' she told him, trying to ignore his last remark.

'Melodie's a good little cook,' the old man informed him eagerly. 'She used to stay here with her grannie and me when she was a little tot, and even then, many's the good parkin she's made, with her grannie's help, of course. Not only parkin either, she can cook anything.'

'Practice makes perfect,' Keith quoted softly, then leaned forward and, under the guise of taking another piece of the cake, murmured close to her ear, 'Does Jed Martin know what a good cook you are?'

She was too surprised to answer for the moment, and anyway her grandfather was already making his own plans. 'You must come and have dinner with us one night,' he told him. 'On Mrs. Bazeley's day off, then you can really see how good a cook Melodie is.'

'Oh, Grampy——' She glanced up at the visitor and caught the glitter of laughter that greeted her protest.

'I wouldn't dream of imposing on your grand-daughter to that extent,' he said, and sounded quite serious.

'You wouldn't *be* imposing,' the old man assured him. 'Melodie likes cooking, you heard her say so.'

He caught her eye at last. '*Would* you mind, Melodie?' he asked quietly, and she shook her head, a sudden impulse urging her on to say what she did.

'No, of course not. I can cook paella or spaghetti as as easily as I can English dishes.'

'Can you?' His voice was unbelievably soft and she could do nothing to avoid his eyes. 'What makes you think I'd want either one or the other?'

'I——' She could feel the colour hot in her cheeks

41

and knew her grandfather was watching curiously. 'I just wondered,' she said lamely at last.

'Well, wonder no more,' he told her. 'If and when I have dinner with you I shall be quite happy with steak and kidney pud or roast beef and Yorkshire.'

'I—I'm sorry.' She had never felt more gauche and schoolgirlish in her life and she wished she had never made that oblique reference to his looks by suggesting a Spanish or Italian dish. She was no wiser, and he had put her firmly in her place.

'I enjoy a good Yorkshire,' the old man told him, probably taking pity on her, Melodie realised. 'You shall have one when you come. Will next Sunday suit you?'

'I'd love to make it next Sunday,' Keith told him, 'but I shall have to delay the invitation for some time, I'm afraid, I have some visitors coming and they'll be here for several weeks, I expect.'

'Ah, some of your family, I suppose,' the old man guessed, and he shook his head.

'No, actually my fian—a friend of mine is coming to stay for a while—with her mother, of course.'

CHAPTER THREE

'His fiancée, he nearly said,' Melodie told Jed the following afternoon as they walked through the spinney, 'and I'm sure he meant it the first time. He wasn't playing some odd sort of joke on me, although I did think so at first.'

'It isn't the sort of thing a man jokes about,' Jed

42

assured her. 'But I'm a bit surprised he said her mother was coming with her.' He pursed a doubtful mouth over the idea. 'No, I don't find that easy to believe.'

'Oh, I don't know,' said Melodie, frowning thoughtfully. 'It could be—after all, he lives there on his own and maybe she isn't the sort of girl to stay in the house alone with him.'

'That's what I can't believe,' Jed told her. 'I'd have thought the sort of woman *he'd* find attractive wouldn't have worried about a chaperone.'

With that impulsive and completely unexpected kiss still fresh in her mind, Melodie was bound to disagree with that, although she could hardly tell him why. 'You don't really know what sort of woman he prefers,' she pointed out instead.

'I could guess.' The round, homely face was set stubbornly, and she realised with a start that he was the first person who had displayed an attitude towards Keith Scott similar to the one she professed to hold. To see it revealed as so blatantly bigoted was most discomfiting and she bit her lip anxiously. 'Anyway,' Jed added, 'he's evidently bent on making an impression, because he's bringing in a full-time cook-housekeeper for the duration of their stay and a maid too.'

'Mrs. Clark?' Melodie guessed, and he nodded. 'No wonder she looked a bit put out when I saw her in the village this morning—she's going to miss all the fun.'

'Likely,' Jed agreed, straight-faced. 'Although I can't see why women make so much fuss about what goes on in somebody else's house.'

'But it's very intriguing,' she protested. 'Of course we're interested.' She was thinking again of that near slip of Keith Scott's, convinced by now that he *was* engaged and busy trying to visualise the type of girl he

43

would be engaged to. She wondered, too, if she had the faintest idea that he was given to kissing his neighbours if they happened to be young, female and passably good-looking.

It was only a few days later that Melodie had the opportunity to discover for herself exactly what Keith Scott's possible fiancée was like, although the meeting could scarcely have been less amicable.

She was walking, as usual, across the meadow on her way to meet Jed, but rather earlier than usual. It was movement off to her right that caught her eye first, and she instinctively turned her head to see what it was.

A horse and rider were making their rather dangerous way through Keith Scott's hastily scattering sheep and heading for the dividing hedge. The rider was not Keith himself this time, although it was the same animal he usually rode. Instead a tall, slim, black-haired woman rode the animal at breakneck speed across the meadow, dispersing the woolly residents in a panic of baaing. She caught her breath when, a second later, horse and rider seemed to take to the air like some giant bird, clearing the hedge easily and continuing their gallop without pause, as if the boundary had been no more than a minor obstacle.

For a moment Melodie stared at them as they headed in her direction and slightly ahead of her, obviously intent on gaining the spinney on the other side. She waved her hands and called out, thinking at first that either she had not been seen or that the rider intended ignoring her. A moment later, however, the black was reined in sharply and the rider sat, slim and straight-backed, in the saddle, waiting for her to approach, making no attempt to meet her half-way.

Melodie guessed that it must be one of Keith Scott's visitors and she was prepared to believe that he had not seen fit to inform the girl that she should not go beyond the dividing hedge. Probably a brief word of explanation and the girl would turn back, she thought, but as she got nearer she was somewhat disconcerted by the unfriendly arrogance with which the girl's dark eyes watched her approach.

Her hair was jet black and her skin a beautiful golden colour. She was, Melodie supposed, rather beautiful if one discounted a certain hardness in the features and the eyes, that were large and slightly tilted at the outer corners. Black and shiny as polished jet, they looked hard and unfriendly as well as arrogant.

She wore well-cut black riding-breeches and boots, and a fine white silk shirt showed off her rather voluptuous figure to advantage. She looked proud and cruel and admittedly rather splendid up there on that big black horse, but definitely not encouraging. That she resented the interruption of her gallop was obvious, but Melodie tried to make allowances.

'Good afternoon.' She smiled up at her, but no responsive smile touched the rather thin-lipped mouth and the eyes were as haughty and unfriendly as ever.

'You wish to address me?'

The English was stilted and strongly accented and, for the moment, Melodie forgave the imperious tone, attributing it to nervousness and probably little knowledge of a strange language. 'I don't suppose you realise it,' she said, 'but you're trespassing by riding across here.'

'Trespassing?' The word was repeated, inexpertly. 'How is this?'

'It—it means you shouldn't be here,' Melodie explained.

Impatience drew the black brows together and her lower lip curled derisively. 'You are telling me that I may not ride here?'

'That's right,' Melodie said, relieved to be understood, but wondering if it helped at all, for there was no relaxation of the haughty stance. 'This land doesn't belong to Mr. Scott, you see,' she went on, 'it belongs to my grandfather. I expect Mr. Scott forgot to mention it to you.'

'How much is your land?'

A hasty interpretation decided Melodie that it was not an offer to buy it and she smiled as she explained. 'From the hedge you came over just now, to the spinney on the other side.'

The girl turned her head and looked around her at the narrow strip of ground that was all that remained of the old Millway land, and the lower lip curled even more disdainfully. 'This—this *remendar* is your land?' An equally derisive gesture with one slim hand added point to the sneer, and Melodie flushed. 'Are you *rústica* that you have so little?' A short, jeering laugh was the last straw and Melodie swallowed her rising anger only with great difficulty. She was accustomed to Keith Scott laughing at her, but never in the way this tall, insolent woman did.

She pointed to the hedge on the western boundary, her mouth set firm. 'Mr. Scott's land ends the other side of that hedge,' she informed the woman, 'and I'd be obliged if you'd go back there now.'

Unmoved by her obvious annoyance, the girl looked across at the spinney and Jed's property beyond. 'And that?' she asked, pointing a finger. 'I may go there?'

'No, you may not,' Melodie told her. 'That belongs to Mr. Martin, and he doesn't like trespassers either.'

The black eyes looked down at her, glittering scornfully. 'You speak for others, huh?'

'I know how my grandfather feels,' Melodie insisted, wishing she was not at such a disadvantage. Standing on the ground she felt very small and insignificant beside the tall, haughty woman on the horse, and she disliked the attitude of her even more than she usually did Keith Scott's. 'I also know that Jed—Mr. Martin dislikes anyone riding over his property and disturbing his sheep as you did those,' she added, glancing back at the field behind her.

The woman's mouth set stubbornly and she looked at Melodie down the length of her arrogant nose. 'And suppose, *rústica*, that I choose to not care how people feel,' she said. 'Who will stop me?'

It was a direct challenge and Melodie faced the fact that she was in no position to do much about it personally. While she held on to her anger determinedly her antagonist gave another short, derisive laugh and her black eyes glittered defiantly as she put her heels to the black, so suddenly that his swift response sent Melodie staggering and almost backwards into the grass.

She stared after the departing rider angrily, maddeningly frustrated at not being able to go after her. Something, she thought, would have to be done about that arrogant newcomer—one resident like that was enough, and at least Keith Scott was not vicious as this woman obviously was.

'Melodie!'

She turned when she heard her name called and saw Keith climbing over the low hedge before leaping the

47

ditch in one long stride. She watched him approach with her eyes still bright with anger, ready to take her revenge on him, wondering how much of the incident he had witnessed.

'You too,' she said, by way of greeting. 'Come right in, it's an invasion.'

His smile remained undisturbed and she knew he was making allowances for her, a fact that did little to help in the circumstances. 'Don't bite my head off,' he told her. 'I only came across to see if you were O.K.'

'Of course I'm all right,' she told him, a bit disconcerted to hear his reason.

He shrugged, still smiling. 'Well, I'm glad I was wrong, but I've no intention of apologising for coming over to find out. You're far too touchy, my girl.'

'I'm not touchy, as you call it,' she denied. 'And I'm *not* your girl!'

He grinned at her in such a way that for one crazy minute she thought he was going to argue the point. 'You definitely are touchy,' he insisted. 'You bridle like a miniature laird every time anyone puts a foot on Millway without your consent.'

'That's not being touchy,' Melodie told him. 'I just don't like all and sundry tramping over our land. Unless of course you think you have every right to,' she added. 'Perhaps you'd like my grandfather and me to move out of Millway and give you and yours the free run of the place.'

He looked at her steadily for a moment and she saw the inevitable amusement lurking deep in his eyes as he shook his head. 'Sarcasm doesn't suit you, Melodie.'

'It——' She stared at him. 'Of all the nerve! You're very often sarcastic to me, I suppose that doesn't count!'

'That's different,' he told her blandly. 'I'm not nearly such a desirable character as you are.' His laugh sent the inevitable shiver along her spine and she wished she could do something about it. 'I saw Maria riding like fury across towards the spinney,' he said, 'and I quite expected to see you hurl yourself bodily in front of Diablo to protect your property.'

'To protect our *remendar*, you mean—whatever that is.' She saw his start of surprise, followed by a smile of understanding. 'I know it's rude,' she went on before he could speak, 'from the way your—your friend said it.'

'Not really rude,' he denied, with a wry smile. 'Although it was rather tactless in the circumstances. It means patch,' he explained when she showed obvious signs of asking.

'She also called me a—a *rústica*,' Melodie informed him, 'and I *don't* need a translation of that, thank you!'

She thought he would have laughed, but instead he frowned and looked quite serious, so that she wondered if she had been too rash in telling him so much. 'I must speak to Maria,' he said.

She looked at him curiously. 'You don't have to make a major issue out of it,' she informed him. 'I just assumed you'd omitted to tell her that you didn't own the whole of Yorkshire.'

'Stop being such a little pussy and pull your claws in,' he told her firmly, while one long finger made a make-believe scratch down one of her cheeks. 'I gather you and Maria didn't see eye to eye.'

'Did you expect us to?' Melodie retorted, evading the caressing finger. 'Don't *do* that!'

'Why not?' The deep blue eyes with their glowing laughter disturbed her strangely.

49

'Because——' She looked away hastily before her cheeks betrayed the reason.

'Did you and Maria argue?' he asked, and she nodded.

'Well, not in the usual sense,' she admitted. 'It was more of an exchange of well camouflaged differences, but you should have told your——'

'Maria,' he interposed quietly. 'Maria Rosita Margarita Santas.'

'Your fiancée?' Melodie ventured, and he eyed her steadily.

'You're presuming an awful lot.'

'It's only a few days ago that you told us she was coming,' she reminded him, 'and you very nearly referred to her as your fiancée.'

'Observant little devil,' he commented. 'It was a slip of the tongue, but it surprised you, I could see that.'

'Nothing of the sort,' she denied hastily. There was something in his voice that should not have been there and she kept her eyes carefully lowered. 'Why on earth should I have been surprised? I don't know anything about you. You could be—be married for all I know. Or care,' she added hastily, and he laughed.

'I'm going from bad to worse, aren't I, Melodie?'

'I've told you,' she insisted, 'it doesn't matter to me if you have a fiancée or—or half a dozen wives. *I* don't care.'

'No?'

'No! But I *do* care that you didn't see fit to let your —Miss Santas know that this property and Jed's was out of bounds to her.'

He cocked a dark brow at her. 'How do you know I didn't, little Miss Righteous?'

Melodie frowned, ignoring the derogatory nickname for the moment, and feeling very uncertain of her ground suddenly. 'I—I naturally assumed you hadn't,' she said.

'Naturally!' The blue eyes held hers steadily, then he laughed again. 'You don't know whether to believe me or not, do you?' he teased.

'I don't know,' she confessed.

'But you'd rather not.'

'I didn't say that,' Melodie denied, 'and I wish you'd stop putting words into my mouth.'

He flicked a brief glance over one shoulder at the returning horse and rider, racing across the field towards them, and smiled. 'You can ask Maria yourself if you like,' he told her. 'It looks very much as if Jed Martin's sent her off with a flea in her ear as well.' He sounded quite unconcerned about it and Melodie wondered if he treated the girl always with that couldn't-care-less attitude.

Maria Santas rode the black at full gallop across the meadow reining him to a halt when she came alongside them. Seeing them together did not please her at all, Melodie realised when she saw the sharp look of dislike in the black eyes and she hastily dismissed the brief moment of pleasure the realisation gave her.

The girl slid gracefully from the saddle and stood beside Keith Scott taking his hand in hers in an oddly shy gesture that was totally unexpected. The way she smiled up at him too could only be called adoring and the black eyes were soft and shining and showed none of the arrogance she had displayed earlier.

She was much taller than Melodie realised and she made her feel smaller than ever, not a desirable sensation in the circumstances. 'Carlos, *amado*.' Her voice too was softer and quieter when she spoke to him in what Melodie recognised as either Spanish or Italian, she was uncertain which, but it excluded Melodie quite pointedly.

The name Carlos puzzled her too, and she saw him recognise it with a knowing smile. 'Speak English, Maria,' he told the girl.

'Carlos——'

'This is Miss Neil, Melodie Neil.' He ignored the threatened argument, and Melodie wondered which of the two of them was more strong-willed, but was not long in doubt. The girl more or less capitulated with a brief nod, and he went on with the introductions as if nothing had happened. 'Melodie, meet Maria Santas.' He did not, she noticed, claim her as his fiancée and she wondered if the omission was deliberate.

Melodie proffered a hand which was merely touched briefly, as if the girl disliked making contact, and she murmured something that Melodie took to be a greeting, then she turned to Keith again and said something in her own tongue.

'Speak English,' he told her, in a tone that brooked no argument. 'It's not polite to use Spanish when Melodie doesn't understand it.' A black brow arched in query at her. 'Or am I doing you an injustice?' he asked. 'Do you speak Spanish, Melodie?' She had just time to shake her head before Maria Santas was off again and in the ensuing spate of Spanish only her own name was intelligible. 'English!' Keith told her sternly, and she made a face complying only reluctantly.

'Melody?' she asked. 'How is that a name? It is a—a *canción*, no? A—a song,' she added hastily.

'That's right,' he told her, in the same tone that he might have used to praise a pupil for being bright. 'But spelled with an i and an e, instead of a y, at the end, it's also a name, Maria.' The blue eyes glowed darkly at Melodie and she could feel the warm colour in her cheeks as she marvelled at the temerity of the man. How dared he flirt so openly with her with his fiancée standing beside him? 'It's a very lovely name,' he added softly, 'and it suits her.'

While she might not have completely understood the words themselves, their meaning was evident enough in his tone and Maria Santas pouted her dislike of the situation. 'I do not think I like you to say such things, *amado,* only to me.'

For once Melodie was in complete agreement with her and she made haste to say so. 'In the circumstances *I* don't like you to say such things either, Mr. Scott,' she told him firmly, and hastily looked away when he laughed softly.

'Only in the circumstances?' he asked softly, and laughed again when she glanced up at him angrily.

'I think you'd better go,' she said.

'*Si,* Carlos, we will go now, huh?' Maria Santas' dark eyes looked deceptively appealing and she laid her black head briefly against his shoulder, again in an oddly touching gesture that surprised Melodie. 'We ride back together.'

She had no intention of leaving without him, that was obvious, and for the moment Melodie wondered how willingly he would comply. Then he nodded. 'We'll ride back together,' he agreed, and lowered one eyelid at Melodie, which she studiously pretended not to see. 'On *my* side of the hedge.'

Maria shrugged as she turned to remount. 'I shall not ride again on this—this *remendar pobre,* do not fear.'

Keith Scott laughed, his eyes glittered wickedly as he looked round at the rich meadow. 'Oh, it's not a poor patch, Maria,' he told her. 'In fact I'd like to buy it one of these days if Melodie will allow her grandfather to sell it to me.'

The jibe did not go unnoticed, and Melodie frowned at him. 'It doesn't depend on what I say, and you know it,' she said. 'My grandfather seems to have taken a liking to you, so I certainly can't speak for him in *that* matter.'

He smiled, his brown face crinkling at the corners of his eyes and mouth. 'I'll have to see him about it one of these days,' he said, and turned to help Maria into the saddle. Seeing her safely settled, he slapped the black sharply on his rump and sent him on his way, watching him go with a smile on his face.

'Carlos!' Maria's voice drifted back to them. '*Despachense*!'

He pulled a wry face and smiled down at Melodie slowly. 'Orders,' he said. 'I'm being told to hurry up.'

Melodie looked at him from under her lashes. 'And do you always do as you're told?' she asked.

He laughed, shaking his head firmly. 'Definitely not,' he told her. 'Only when it suits me to, and it does —at the moment.' She was not quite certain what that rather enigmatic qualification was meant to convey, but she would not have dreamed of asking him, so she merely nodded as if she understood perfectly. 'I'll see you again, Melodie.'

Although she wished to avoid him if possible the following day, Melodie found herself in a position where she had little choice. She had been shopping in the village and she was on her way back when Keith

Scott's big black car pulled up alongside her and he leaned over to open the passenger seat door.

'Hop in,' he told her, 'I'll run you back.' He held out a hand for the shopping basket and she had little option but to do as he said.

'Thank you.'

'You don't look very pleased to see me,' he told her. 'With all that shopping I'd have thought you'd have welcomed anybody with transport, even me.'

'I've said I'm grateful,' she said. 'I—I just wondered if you were alone, that's all, but as you are I suppose it's O.K.'

'For heaven's sake, what difference does that make?' She didn't answer and he laughed. 'If you're worried about Maria, she and her mother have gone shopping in Cydale.' Above the white shirt he wore his face looked even more brown than usual and the blue eyes even more out of place. She was aware, too, that they flicked briefly and curiously in her direction as if he was watching for her reaction to the information.

His reference to Maria's absence, she felt, hinted rather at conspiracy, as if he was waiting for her to relax and be more at ease with him because his fiancée was conveniently out of the way, and she resented the implication. Having a fiancée, she thought, seemed not to cramp his style at all, and it was time he was reminded of the fact.

'Shopping for a trousseau?' she asked quietly, hoping to show him once and for all that she was not interested in competing with Maria Santas.

'No.' He answered quietly enough, but she thought the mention of a trousseau displeased him or perhaps disconcerted him for the moment, and she could not help feeling mildly pleased with herself.

55

'Oh, I thought Miss Santas might have been over here for the wedding.' She looked at him with wide, green eyes that appeared deceptively mild and innocent. 'You did tell my grandfather Miss Santas was your fiancée, didn't you?' she asked. 'Or at least you said that your fiancée and her mother were coming to stay with you.'

'You said so,' he corrected her quietly. 'I amended the statement, if you remember.'

'Yes, you did.'

'But you didn't believe me?'

'I didn't say so,' Melodie denied, wondering if she had started something she would be sorry about. 'I wasn't sure if you'd changed your mind because Miss Santas isn't your fiancée, or because you have a fiancée and she isn't it.'

He laughed, raising appealing eyes to heaven. 'I suppose you know what you're talking about,' he told her, 'and I *think* I do. You're implying that there are probably two ladies—shall we say—involved?—and at the moment you're not sure which one Maria is.'

'It's no concern of mine *who* she is,' she declared.

'Exactly!' He turned his head and grinned at her wryly. 'But it would be much more interesting to credit me with a harem, wouldn't it? You'd find it much more in character, wouldn't you, Melodie?'

'I'm—I'm not sure what *is* in character,' she confessed, and he shook his head.

'But it doesn't stop you jumping to conclusions.'

'I did *not*,' she denied indignantly. 'You were the one who brought up the subject of—of a harem, not me. I assumed Miss Santas was your fiancée.'

'And that she'd come over here to marry me.'

'Well, it—it seemed a reasonable assumption,' she

56

said, and he turned a brief but steady gaze on her.

'Are you anxious to see me married off, Melodie?' he asked, and laughed softly when she did not immediately reply.

He drew up some yards short of the gates into Millway and made no attempt to open the door but turned in his seat to face her, his gaze both amused and curious. 'I—I'm not particularly interested either way,' she told him, thinking she should get out of the car and leave him, but held there by something she could not explain for the life of her. 'Your affairs are nothing to do with me, Mr. Scott.'

'Affairs?' He tilted a black brow at her, his eyes glinting wickedly. 'So you do suspect me of—well, of what, I wonder?'

'It's your own fault,' she accused, 'you put words into my mouth.'

He laughed softly and she coped yet again with that trickle of excitement that coursed along her spine. 'It's such a lovely mouth too,' he said, his gaze fixed on that feature as if it fascinated him.

'I think I'd better go,' she said, and turned away to open the door, but he leaned across and held it closed, much too close for comfort.

'If I promise not to tease you will you stay and talk to me?' he asked, and she could do nothing to stop the smile that answered him. 'And just for once,' he begged, seeing her won over, 'could you manage to feel friendly enough disposed towards me to call me Keith?'

Melodie looked at him curiously, then turned again to open the door, this time succeeding before he could stop her. 'I must go,' she told him. 'I can walk the last few yards, thank you.'

He allowed her to get out, then left his own seat and walked with her the few yards to the gate. She went in through the gate and he stood on the other side of it, reaching out for one of her hands to keep her there.

'Why, Melodie? Why won't you talk to me for a while?'

'I—I don't know,' she confessed.

'Then stay.' The blue eyes tempted her and she looked away hastily, but stayed where she was on the other side of the gate with his hand holding her free one.

'Mr. Scott——'

'Keith.'

She looked at him again, her curiosity aroused again. '*Is* your name Keith?' she asked. 'Miss Santas called you Carlos.'

He laughed softly, recognising her curiosity and not resenting it. 'Maria finds English very difficult to get her tongue round sometimes,' he told her, 'and Keith isn't the easiest name to pronounce with a Spanish tongue.'

'Oh, I see.'

He chuckled. 'I don't think you do,' he said, 'but I wish you'd call me Keith just the same.'

'In the circumstances, I'm not sure it's a very good idea,' she said.

'What circumstances, for heaven's sake?'

'Well—Miss Santas didn't like me very much, and she'd like me even less if she knew I was on first name terms with you.'

'Maria,' he said firmly, 'has no concern in what I want. She'll have to accept things as I want them, and like it.'

'Well, of all the arrogant——!' She looked at him

58

for a moment, then shook her head, pulling her hand free of his as if she had only just realised he still held it. 'I wouldn't be engaged to you for all the tea in China,' she declared. 'Just who *are* you, Mr. Keith Scott, that you can lay down the law to a woman like Maria Santas and get away with it?'

The blue eyes, so startling in his brown face, glittered with laughter at her curiosity. 'I'm Keith Scott,' he informed her solemnly. 'Farmer and landowner of this parish.'

'But you're not English.' She had not meant it to sound quite so much like an accusation, and she wasn't in the least surprised when he laughed.

'You're a curious little monkey, aren't you?' he said. 'Am I condemned if I admit it?'

'Not condemned,' Melodie told him, disliking the air of patronage. 'But it would mean that you've been —well, living here under a false name, and *that* doesn't give a very good impression.'

'It's not a false name,' he denied, and she frowned when he laughed again, enjoying her confusion.

'But you said you're not British,' she insisted, 'and Keith sounds British enough.'

'Ah well, you see, I'm an eldest son, and the eldest son in our family is *always* called Keith, after my great-great-granddaddy.'

'All right,' she said resignedly. 'I give up. What nationality are you? American?'

He did not sound American, but that was not an infallible way to judge, if he had spent quite a lot of time in England. Too late she remembered Jed's information about the letters he received, passed on from the busy Mrs. Clark.

'Argentinian,' he said, and looked surprised when

she smiled wryly.

'Of course!'

'Why of course?'

'News,' she said darkly, 'travels.'

'Apparently.'

'Only——' She looked puzzled again. 'Well, shouldn't you have a Spanish name or something?'

His smile was wide and dazzling in the brown face. 'I have,' he said, confounding her further. 'Keith Carlos Ramon Scott, if you wish to be very precise about it, and I'm sure you do.'

'Oh—I see.'

'Are you sure?' he taunted, and she stuck out her chin at him.

'Yes, I'm sure. You're half and half.'

He laughed then, louder than ever. Standing by the gate as he was, he was in the shadow of a tree that grew beside it and his face looked darker than ever, only those deep blue eyes were out of place in features that otherwise looked purely Spanish.

'You're not quite right,' he told her, 'but it's a good guess. There's only a very little dash of English blood left. Or at least British to be strictly honest.'

'But you speak English perfectly, you even speak—speak slang.'

'I've spent a large part of my life over here,' he told her. 'Most of my life since I was eleven when I came over to school, in that time anyone could pick up a language.'

'You sound like Methuselah,' she retorted, and he grinned.

'Maybe I am to you,' he told her with a grin.

'Oh, don't be so ridiculous!' She felt suddenly shy, realising how intimate their conversation had become,

60

and the way he was looking at her did nothing to help her think clearly. It was high time she took the shopping back to the house, and returned to normality.

'I—I must be going,' she told him. 'Grampy will be waiting for his tea.'

He glanced at his watch, 'Not yet he won't,' he argued, and added something in Spanish which made her look at him suspiciously.

'What are you saying?' she asked.

'Nothing you'd take very kindly to at the moment, *enamorada*,' he told her softly, and laughed.

'You told Miss Santas it was rude to speak Spanish when I didn't understand it,' she reminded him. 'The same applies to you, surely. Or are you exempt from the rules?'

'But of course!'

'Of course,' she echoed, and looked at him from under her lashes, speculating how rash she was being. 'I was always under the impression that Spanish men were very good-mannered,' she told him. 'Obviously you're exempt from that too.'

'Ah, but you forget my great-great-granddaddy,' he reminded her solemnly. 'He wasn't a Spanish gentleman, you know. He left Scotland a hundred years ago with a wife and two sons, to seek his fortune, and started with a few cattle and a miserable patch of land. We've become South American by absorption and marriage, but only very slowly. I'm no gallant Spanish don, Melodie, I'm a farmer.'

Melodie looked at him steadily for a moment, seeing that first Keith Scott's blue eyes in the otherwise Spanish face. 'No matter what you say,' she told him, 'I can recognise pride when I see it.'

He smiled then, and the whiteness of it in the brown

61

face never failed to fascinate her. 'Only you prefer to call it arrogance, don't you?' he asked, and shrugged. 'Well, you're probably right. Being born with several square miles of pampas and God knows how many head of cattle as your inheritance can give one a feeling of pride, arrogance if you like, and I suppose even twenty or so years in England can't alter that.'

'I—I didn't mean to criticise,' she assured him, fearing she'd gone too far, but he laughed good-naturedly.

'Now don't spoil it by apologising,' he told her. 'It wouldn't be you if you didn't say exactly what you thought.'

'I didn't intend being rude, just the same.'

He cocked a curious brow at her and smiled. 'You are honest,' he said. 'Disconcertingly so sometimes. Are you as frank with Jed Martin as you are with me?'

The question about Jed was so unexpected that she stared at him for a moment before answering.

'I—I can't think what Jed has to do with it,' she said.

'Aren't you thinking of marrying him soon?'

She merely blinked, too startled to reply for the moment. 'I don't know,' she managed at last. 'And I don't really see how it concerns anyone but Jed and me if—well, if it does happen.'

'Just friendly curiosity,' he told her with a smile. 'Like you asking about Maria's trousseau.'

'Oh, I see. A case of you started it.' She felt her cheeks pink and decided that at least one of them should apologise. 'Well, I'm sorry I was so curious, but you didn't have to tell me the rest—about yourself,' she added in case there should be any doubt.

'But you asked me.' He dared her to deny it and when she did not he shook his head in self-reproach.

'No, perhaps that was unfair of me. A woman is entitled to be curious, it's all part of her charm, and I'm flattered that you were interested enough to want to know.'

Melodie saw suddenly that he would be getting quite the wrong impression if she did not quickly put him right. 'I was only normally curious,' she told him. 'It had nothing to do with the fact that I'm a woman, and certainly it wasn't because—well, for the reason you're implying.'

He shook his head slowly, his expression crestfallen and, but for the laughter in his eyes, she would have believed him serious. 'I'm disappointed,' he said. 'I'm bitterly disappointed, Melodie.'

'Oh, don't be so——' She bit her lip, disturbed by a sudden strange feeling of intimacy in his teasing, and she had not realised how close he was standing; there was only inches between them.

'Aah! Don't say anything you'll be sorry for,' he warned, and his brown face crinkled into a smile.

'Stop talking to me as if I were Maria,' Melodie told him. '*I* shan't gaze at you adoringly and do as you tell me!'

He laughed as if the idea amused him. 'Does she do as I tell her?' he asked, and Melodie nodded firmly.

'She'll do anything to please you, you must be perfectly well aware of that.'

'And you'd tell me to go to hell, wouldn't you, Melodie?'

She nodded again, the violence of the gesture further dishevelling her red hair. 'Yes, I would; I don't believe in being a doormat to any man.'

He laughed, shaking his head, a deep and continuous roar of mirth that was both loud and disconcerting.

'Oh, Melodie,' he managed at last, 'you're wonderful!'

'I'm glad you find it amusing,' she told him, 'but I can't see why you should.'

'Can't you?' He looked at her wickedly. 'You think you can foresee exactly how you'll behave when it comes to the point,' he told her, 'but I'll bet every acre I own that when you *really* fall in love, you'll be as amenable, or more so, than Maria or anyone else.'

'Oh no, I won't,' she declared, firmly convinced. 'I have a mind of my own.'

'Mmm, I know.' He swept his gaze over her in one expressive gesture that not only brought swift colour to her face but did disturbing things to her pulse as well. Then before she realised what he meant to do, a grip as strong as steel pulled her hard against the wooden gate and his mouth was on hers, stilling any protest she might have made, and setting into motion a wild and uncontrollable hammering under her ribs.

She should have been objecting, she realised several moments later when he released her, but she was too stunned for the moment to do anything more than cling to the gate with one hand while her other still held fast to the basket. Her eyes, wide and green, stared at him and she realised it was the second time he had caught her unawares like that, wishing she could find words to tell him how she felt about it.

Instead she had still not found her tongue when he laughed softly and ruffled his fingers through her hair, bending his head again briefly to brush her mouth with his before he turned away and strode back towards his car. He turned after a second or two and raised one hand in a casual salute, his brown face creased into a smile.

'*Adios*, little copper-nob,' he called.

CHAPTER FOUR

MELODIE was tidying the small table beside her grandfather's chair, and she was aware that he had been watching her curiously for some time. She had said nothing to him about her meeting with Keith, especially its outcome, because she knew he would misconstrue the whole thing and make far more of it than there was.

The shrewd old eyes followed her progress round the room as she dusted the sideboard. 'Are you still seeing Jed Martin?' he asked suddenly—so suddenly that she paused in her dusting and frowned at him curiously.

'Yes, of course I'm still seeing him. Why?'

The dark eyes, sharp in his sunken face, looked knowing. 'I just wondered,' he said. 'I haven't heard much about him lately.'

'Grampy, you know I've never talked much about Jed,' she told him. 'Why should I suddenly start now?'

'No, I suppose you haven't,' the old man acknowledged. 'Are you ashamed of him?'

'Ashamed of him?' She stared for a moment, too stunned to reply, wondering where on earth he could have got such an idea from. 'No, of course I'm not ashamed of him, how on earth can you ask such a thing? You've never even met Jed.'

'Precisely,' her grandfather retorted. 'I reckon it's time I did.'

She remembered Jed's suggestion, some days ago,

that he should come to the house and meet the old man, and thought this was probably as good an opportunity as any to mention the matter. Knowing her grandfather it was quite possible he would immediately see the reason behind the suggestion.

'Jed would like to meet you,' she told him. 'As a matter of fact he said as much a few days ago.'

'And you didn't say anything.'

'I—I forgot,' she confessed, and the old man tut-tutted.

'Forgot!'

'I did,' Melodie insisted. 'Anyway, shall I ask him to come to dinner on Sunday?'

'Suits me,' her grandfather said.

'Shall I ask him to bring Michael?'

'Michael?' He frowned for a moment, then remembered. 'Oh yes, his lad.' He looked at her with what she always called his sly look. 'Best not,' he told her. 'If a man's coming courting he doesn't want a little lad along with him.'

'Coming——' Melodie looked at him warily.

'He *is* courting you, isn't he?' the old man demanded. 'I'd say meeting a lass practically every day for nearly a year was courting her.'

'Yes—yes, I suppose it is,' she allowed, still rather suspicious of his sudden desire to meet Jed. If she knew her grandfather as well as she thought she did, he was bound to make some pretty pointed remarks concerning Jed's intentions towards her, even if Jed himself did not say anything, and she was not at all sure that she wanted to be precipitated into anything more definite yet. For one thing, she would never consider leaving him while he was still so ill.

'Then it's high time I met him,' the old man declared

firmly. 'I'm standing in for your parents while you're here with me, and if this feller's serious I should meet him and give him the once-over.'

'Oh, Grampy!' Embarrassment and laughter battled for precedence, but eventually the determinedly stubborn look on his face proved too much for her and she burst into laughter, shaking her head over him, her eyes bright with it. 'You're a conniving old man,' she declared, 'but please don't meet Jed with that fierce Victorian papa face or he'll probably sell up and move out of the county!'

'Not if he loves you, he won't,' her grandfather told her, and cocked a brow at her, an expression that looked oddly wicked in his wrinkled old face. 'He *does* love you, I suppose?'

Melodie laughed again; uncertain but reluctant to admit it. 'I suppose so,' she said, 'although he's never actually said so in as many words.'

'Then he's slow,' he declared stoutly, 'and he'd best make a move before some other feller beats him to it.'

'Some——' She realised suddenly who the some other feller was that he had in mind and she shook her head, returning to her dusting rather than face the speculative look in his eyes as he watched her. 'That's very unlikely, Grampy,' she told him, 'and please leave me to manage my own life. I know what I'm doing.'

'You're a rare woman if you do,' the old man retorted. He was silent for a few minutes and Melodie was hopeful that he had perhaps dozed off to sleep. She was just leaving the room, as quietly as she could when he spoke again, and she turned to see him watching her closely. 'How do you get along with young Scott?' he asked.

Melodie suppressed a sigh that recognised the inevitable. Her grandfather never left a subject until he had exhausted its possibilities. 'I get along fairly well with him,' she said cautiously. 'Why? What makes you ask that?'

'Now he's a feller who'd not waste time,' her grandfather informed her. 'He'd not dilly and dally, he knows his own mind, does that one.'

'Really?' The implication was so obvious there was no point in pretending ignorance, so she took the bull by the horns and looked at him steadily. 'Well, Mr. Scott is unlikely to be a candidate for my hand, as you seem to think, because for one thing he already has a fiancée, remember?'

'So you said,' the old man agreed, and sounded startlingly like Keith Scott himself.

'But you heard him,' she protested.

'I heard him change his mind half way,' the old man retorted, and added, 'What's that woman like who's staying with him?'

'I told you,' Melodie said. 'A glamorous South American who despises our little bit of land.'

'She doesn't sound like his cup of tea,' he declared. 'And there's one thing you didn't mention, that I'd have thought would be the first thing a woman would have noticed. You said naught about a ring.'

'A ring?' Melodie tried hard to picture again those long slim hands waving disdainfully round the remaining Millway land, or curled possessively round Keith Scott's. There had been no ring that she remembered and she wondered why the idea made her heart give such a skip, as if it pleased her. The significance of there being no ring had, until now, escaped her. 'I—I didn't notice a ring,' she confessed.

'Then there wasn't one,' her grandfather stated confidently. 'Women always notice things like that.'

'I suppose so.' She considered it for a moment thoughtfully. 'Ah well,' she said at last, 'maybe customs are different in Argentina.'

'And maybe that's why he changed his mind and corrected himself,' he told her, 'because he *isn't* engaged to her.'

'Maybe.' She remembered how evasive Keith had been on the subject of Maria Santas. 'Anyway,' she added, with the firm intention of closing the subject, 'it's nothing to do with us either way.'

'It's interesting.'

'Not to me,' Melodie insisted. 'Now try and get some sleep, Grampy, you'll be overtired.'

'No, I won't,' he argued. 'And don't tell me you're not interested in anything to do with young Scott. He's the kind of man any woman would be interested in, and you're no different from the rest, my girl.'

Jed accepted the invitation for Sunday, but seemed a little unsure if he should come or not, saying that he perhaps shouldn't impose when the old man was so ill. Melodie insisted, a bit impatiently she knew, for it seemed almost as if he was reluctant to meet the old man now that it came to the point.

Sunday was wet right from the start when Melodie looked out of her window first thing, and she pulled a face at the grey, heavy-looking sky, hoping it wasn't an omen to set the seal on the rest of the day. She anticipated some reluctance on Jed's part about meeting her grandfather, because he was not an outgoing man and often gave the impression, on first meeting, of being surly and unfriendly, while the old man on the other hand was much more of an extrovert and had little patience with shyness.

Mrs. Bazeley was visiting her sister for the weekend and Melodie was cooking the meal, consequently she was in the kitchen when Jed arrived and met him at the door looking more than usually flushed from the heat of the oven. He looked smart but rather uncomfortable in a dark grey suit and tie with a blue shirt, and so grave-faced she knew he was terribly nervous.

He shook raindrops from his head as he ran into the house and Melodie made a wry face at the still falling rain. 'It's a filthy day,' she said. 'Look how wet you are even just coming from the car.'

'It's the wrong time of year too,' Jed agreed, more practical. 'We could have done with this in the spring.' He did no more than brush his lips lightly against her cheek, but he did put an arm around her shoulders to hug her close for a moment as they walked towards the sitting-room.

Her grandfather looked up, his shrewd eyes narrowed expectantly, but he smiled a welcome at Jed when Melodie introduced them. 'Now can I leave you two to talk?' she said after a few minutes. 'I have the dinner to cook, and I don't want anything to spoil.' It was, in a way, a coward's way out, but she hated the idea of being there while her grandfather made the inevitable reference to their relationship, although she ought probably to have stayed and given support to Jed.

Dinner was a passable success, although Jed was no great conversationalist and his response to her grandfather's remark that she was an excellent cook evoked no more than a polite agreement, and certainly none of the enthusiasm that Keith Scott had displayed in the same circumstances. She caught her grand-

70

father's eye and noted the raised brow, and she was mildly disappointed, but not really surprised. Jed was not a man of many words.

She was surprised, however, when he followed her into the kitchen after dinner when she carried out the last of the dishes. He carefully closed the door behind him and she turned to look at him, smiling enquiringly. 'Have you come to dry up?' she asked, knowing he would not take her seriously. He was silent for so long that she turned away again and tied an apron over her dress and frothed up a sinkful of soapy suds before he answered her.

'I wanted to talk to you alone, Melly.' The round homely face was serious as always when she turned her back on the piled up dishes in the sink and looked at him curiously, wiping her soapy hands absently on her apron.

'You see me alone almost every day,' she reminded him.

'Aye but not like this,' he told her. 'I've seen your grandfather, Melly, and he says we can get engaged.'

It was typical of Jed, she thought a little breathlessly, to tell her that her grandfather had agreed to their engagement before he had even asked her. She turned back to the sink, unable to do anything about the feeling of disappointment that easily outdid the excitement of the occasion. 'Do I take that as a proposal?' she asked quietly, and sensed rather than heard him move behind her.

'You know how I feel, Melly.'

He stood just behind her, but he made no move to touch her and she wondered, for one delirious second, if he was afraid of getting soapsuds on his good suit. 'I'm not sure I do, Jed.' Her hands trembled a little as

71

she washed the dishes and she supposed she did feel some stirring pleasure at the idea of having Jed at last say where he stood, but the moment was nowhere near as exciting as she had always anticipated it would be. She had never visualised receiving a proposal of marriage in the kitchen, for one thing, up to her elbows in soapsuds and dirty dishes.

Not that anything he had said so far could be strictly called a proposal, but the setting was not right at all. Jed's manner, too, left a lot to be desired when it came to being romantic. She knew he was frowning, even without looking at him.

'Oh, Melly, you know I'm no good at making pretty speeches.'

'Not even to the extent of saying you love me?' Melodie asked, and heard him sigh.

'You *know* I love you—I'm going to marry you, aren't I?'

She was silent for a while, turning the things up to drain, and drying her hands carefully. 'I *don't* know, Jed.' Her desire to have the occasion made more romantic, she realised, probably made her appear capricious, but she could not help that. It was all so different from what she had expected and she could not help being disappointed.

Jed turned her round to face him and she could see the blank look of disbelief in his eyes when he looked at her. 'What do you mean? You don't know.'

'You've never said you love me,' she told him.

'Do I have to?'

She looked down at her hands clasped together on his chest, knowing she was being unfair. 'If you want me to marry you,' she said, and he stared at her stubbornly.

'Oh, I see—you're making conditions.' He dropped his hands and looked, if anything, faintly sheepish. 'Well, I thought I knew you and I thought you knew me well enough,' he said. 'I've been a bit of a fool, haven't I?'

'Oh no, Jed!' She realised now that her offhand manner had not only hurt him but made him think she cared nothing for him, and that simply wasn't true. She could not imagine Jed not being there, with his solid good sense and understanding. It might not have been love she felt for him, not the kind of romantic love that she had always imagined would sweep her off her feet, but she would go a long way before she found anyone more kind, gentle and dependable than Jed.

He was looking at her hopefully, his round face and light hair giving him an oddly pathetic look. 'You mean you're not turning me down, Melly?'

'I—I'm sorry I was so mean, Jed.' She turned away from him when he would have taken her arms again, unable to face him while she sorted out her own chaotic reasoning. 'I—I don't really love you,' she confessed. 'Not in the usual way, I want you to know that, but I do care for you in—well, in a different sort of way.'

He turned her round to face him again then and she knew he was content to accept all she could offer, even if it wasn't a romantic kind of love. 'I just want to marry you,' he said. 'Never mind the *way* you love me, Melly, I'll settle for that.'

'You're sure it's—it's enough?' She traced the outline of a lapel, not wanting to look at him yet, feeling she was still being a bit unfair.

He smiled, a rare smile that made his homely face look much younger. 'It's enough,' he told her, and produced a small box from his pocket with a gesture that was more flamboyant than anything she had seen him do yet.

A warm red ruby sat surrounded by several small but perfect diamonds that glinted and shone even in the dull light, the gold ring itself bright and glowing against the black velvet, and Melodie drew a sharp breath at the unexpected sight of it.

'Do you like it?'

She nodded, feeling rather like crying to think that he had chosen anything so beautiful for her. 'It's—it's beautiful, Jed!'

He took her left hand and slid the ring on to the third finger, finding it rather a loose fit. 'Never mind,' he told her, 'we can have it made smaller. You have such small hands.'

'Oh, that's a minor trouble,' she said. 'It's very lovely and we can quite easily have a bridge-clip put in to make it smaller.' She was not very fond of jewellery as a rule, but it would not do to feel the same way about an engagement ring, and it must have cost Jed a great deal of money.

'I suppose Aunt Maud had much bigger hands,' he told her, and Melodie looked at him curiously.

'Aunt——'

'My mother's sister,' he explained. 'The ring was hers originally, and she left it to me along with a lot of other things, in her will. It's quite a good one, I believe.'

'Oh, yes I can see it is,' Melodie said faintly. It was not that she had anything against family rings being handed on, but somehow it was rather a blow to discover that Jed had not after all chosen it specially for her as she had thought. Perhaps being a wife to a

74

farmer like Jed, involved accepting things like un-romantic proposals and heirloom rings, and for the first time since he had known him, she wondered what his first wife had been like.

Her grandfather duly admired the ring and pulled her face down to kiss her gently when they broke the news to him a few minutes later. He held her hands and looked at her as if he sensed some of her doubts. 'You know I wish you every happiness, my lass,' he told her softly in his dry voice. 'But don't be in too much of a hurry to take the next step, hmm?'

'No, of course not, Grampy.' She kissed him gently, and thought she had not misinterpreted the reason for his warning. It had nothing to do with selfish motives, she felt sure, but stemmed from a very real fear of seeing her do the wrong thing.

It was a couple of hours later, when she was seeing Jed out, that they heard a car stop outside and a moment later a short rat-a-tat-tat on the front door.

'Now who on earth can that be?' Jed asked while Melodie went to answer the summons.

She opened the door and was not altogether sur-prised to see Keith Scott standing on the step look-ing, for him, very apologetic. He did not greet her with his customary smile but looked at her as if he won-dered what his reception was going to be, and she could not restrain the smile that came to her lips when she saw him.

'Hello,' she said.

'I'm sorry to trouble you, Melodie,' he told her, his eyes noting Jed standing in the hall behind her and frowning over the sight of him. 'Especially on a Sun-day evening, but Doctor Grieve is away for the day and

his locum's miles away. I know you're a nurse and
——' She signed to him to come in out of the rain,
and he stepped into the hall.

'Is someone ill?' she asked.

He shrugged and made a face. 'I wish I knew,' he
confessed. 'It's Señora—Mrs. Santas, Maria's mother,
she's had a fainting fit of some kind and Maria's
getting worked up about it.' The blue eyes were more
humble than she had ever known them and Melodie
knew she would be going with him even before he
asked her to. 'Melodie, *would* you come and see if it's
really worth getting the locum over or if——' He
stopped short, and shook his head. 'I don't know much
about fainting fits,' he said, 'and better safe than
sorry.'

'Yes, yes, of course I'll do what I can.' She reached
for her coat from the hall-stand and looked at Jed
apologetically. 'I ought to go now, Jed, in case it's
anything that needs a doctor.' Without waiting for him
to say anything she spoke over her shoulder to Keith.
'I'll just let Grampy know where I'll be.'

Jed frowned his displeasure as she opened the
sitting-room door, the dislike as much for the man
who had asked for her help as for the fact that she had
been called upon at all. 'Surely the doctor would be
better,' he said shortly. 'It's not that far into Cydale
and Doctor Morton's always willing to come out.'

'Oh, Jed, I don't mind really,' Melodie assured
him. 'And it isn't worth bringing Doctor Morton all
out here unless it is serious, and I can soon tell that I
expect.'

'Well, I *do* mind,' he told her, unexpectedly aggres-
sive, and she was aware of Keith Scott's curiosity.

'But you were just going home anyway,' she reminded him, a little unkindly perhaps, 'so it doesn't really make any difference, does it, Jed?

'But you're not the district nurse to be called by all and sundry,' he objected, and Melodie sighed.

'Jed, I'm a nurse, someone is unwell and I may be able to help, I won't know until I get there, and it's no trouble for me to go and look, so let's not argue anymore about it.'

She went into the sitting-room, aware of her grandfather's curious gaze, having heard the preceding conversation. 'I have to go out for a little while, Grampy,' she explained, collecting a thermometer from the medicine table. 'I won't be very long.'

He nodded approval. 'You go on, lass, I'll be perfectly O.K. on my own for a while.'

Melodie kissed the top of his head and tucked the blanket in around him. 'Try to sleep, Grampy, and I'll be as quick as I can.'

The old man peered past her to where Jed hovered, gloomily, in the hall. 'Doesn't your new fiancé approve of your errand of mercy?' he asked in a stage whisper, and Melodie merely frowned at him discouragingly.

'I won't be very long,' she repeated, but smiled reproachfully at him as she closed the door.

Jed looked at the intruder as if he suspected him of some vile trick. 'At least let me drive you over there,' he said, but Melodie shook her head.

'That would be silly, Jed, when Mr. Scott can take me and bring me back.'

He looked down at the diamond and ruby ring she still wore, loosely, on her left hand. 'Don't lose that ring,' he told her. 'Remember it's loose.'

She saw Keith's eyes fixed on the ring briefly before

she removed it, and thought there was more than a hint of the usual laughter in them, as if he recognised Jed's remark for what it was. A way of showing him that they were now engaged and not to forget it.

She hastily tore off a tiny piece of tissue paper from a piece she found in a drawer and wrapped the ring before putting it in her purse. 'There,' she said, 'that should be safe enough in there until I can have it made smaller.'

'Shall we go?' Keith asked, and she nodded, sparing another moment for Jed before they left the house together.

She tiptoed and kissed him lightly beside his mouth. 'I'll see you tomorrow, Jed.'

He nodded, still not very pleased about the turn of events, and watched her climb into Keith Scott's car, but he did not return the wave she gave him as they drove off. Jed, she decided, was showing an entirely new side to his character. She had never known him to sulk before, but he was very definitely sulking now, unless she was very much mistaken.

The rain had stopped for a moment, but the car sent great sprays of water into the air as they drove along the narrow road to Crowe's, and it looked as if there would be more rain before nightfall. Her companion was unusually silent and she wondered if the sickness of his prospective mother-in-law worried him more than he admitted. The dark face showed no sign of worry and his hands on the wheel revealed no tension or anxiety, but there must be some reason for his being so quiet.

'Are congratulations in order?'

The question coming so suddenly after a long silence made her start. 'Congratulations?'

The blue eyes flicked briefly in her direction and he

smiled. 'I suppose you're going to tell me that it's none of my business,' he guessed, 'but I couldn't very well miss that bit of by-play about the ring and I *did* notice which finger you were wearing it on.'

'It's no secret,' Melodie told him, oddly reluctant to discuss it. 'Jed gave me the ring this afternoon.'

'I see. Then congratulations are in order—to Jed, at least.'

'Not to——' she began, and he laughed, setting her toes tingling and the pulse in her temple skipping wildly.

'It's surely not the done thing to congratulate the woman, is it?' he asked. 'I always thought it was considered rather tactless, like congratulating a huntress on making a kill.'

Melodie flushed, turning reproachful eyes on him. 'No matter what you may think,' she told him, 'I didn't do any hunting, and there was no kill.'

Another brief glance swept over her face and he smiled. 'You'd never have to hunt,' he said softly. 'There'd be too many willing victims waiting to be led like lambs to the slaughter.'

Despite the embarrassment she felt at the rather exaggerated compliment, she could not restrain a smile. 'You make me sound like Helen of Troy,' she said. 'And far from my having a whole string of boy-friends, Jed's the only one now.'

'But that's only because you've been buried out here for the past year,' he told her. 'There hasn't been much competition for him, has there?' He was silent for a moment, then she saw him smile. 'If you were mine,' he said, 'I'd take you out more and show you off instead of keeping you practically in purdah.'

She laughed softly, meeting his eyes for a brief,

breathless second. 'And risk having me run off with someone else?' she said.

He smiled, slowly, and his voice had a depth and timbre she had never heard before so that she curled her fingers into her palms at the sound of it. 'I'd make sure you didn't *want* to run off with anyone else,' he told her.

They were already turning into the short driveway at Crowe's and she could not even think of a single word to answer him, carefully avoiding his eyes as he opened the car door for her.

The old farmhouse had changed a great deal since old Mr. Crowe's day. A face-lift with paint and cement had given it a more cared-for look and the windows were bright and clean, which the old man never bothered about. It looked, in fact, far more of a home now and much more attractive.

A woman came into the hall when they came in, but she saw that her employer had company and disappeared again without a word. 'Mrs. Santas is upstairs,' Keith explained. 'I thought it was best if she lay down.'

Melodie frowned, her professional interest taking over. 'That depends,' she told him. 'Was she pale?'

He led the way up the wide carpeted stairs and along a landing to a door at the end. 'No,' he said, as if it required some thought to answer correctly. 'Actually she was fur—rather angry and her face was red immediately before and I thought——' He shrugged. 'I hope I'm not wasting your time,' he added.

Something in his manner puzzled her, and she thought he had been more frank than he intended when he told her that Mrs. Santas had been angry. There had been something in the way he spoke at the house too, and she looked at him curiously as he opened the bedroom door.

There were two women in the room, one was Maria Santas and the other an older, even tighter-lipped version with greying hair, obviously her mother. They both regarded Melodie with suspicion and the elder one flicked a look at Keith that should have shrivelled him on the spot.

'*A médico?*' she demanded, and it was easy to follow her meaning. If this was her patient, however, Melodie could see little to cause concern, although the woman was surrounded by pillows and a quilt lay across her legs. The rather gaunt face still looked flushed and, as Keith had almost said, furiously angry.

Maria Santas was on her feet and she looked at Melodie narrow-eyed before turning to her mother and apparently explaining who she was. That the description was far from complimentary was obvious from the older woman's expression.

Maria turned to Melodie again, her eyes glowing scornfully. 'You go now,' she told her, and Melodie would have been only too happy to comply, but Keith Scott still had a hand on her arm and his fingers tightened perceptibly at the terse order.

'I asked Melodie to come here, Maria,' he told the girl, 'because she's a nurse and Doctor Grieve is away. I thought your mother needed help.' He glanced at the woman on the bed. 'I can see now that I need not have troubled Melodie at all.'

From her expression it was evident that Mrs. Santas understood English at least as well as her daughter did, but she replied in Spanish, which Keith immediately translated. 'Mrs. Santas thanks you for coming,' he told her, 'but she would not dream of troubling anyone

81

with her health except a doctor.'

'Doesn't she understand I'm a nurse?' Melodie asked, and before he could reply Maria took a hand again, her black eyes glittering angrily.

'We do not need you,' she said. 'You can go.'

'Maria!' His voice was thunderous and Maria visibly flinched before it. 'Melodie came over here at my request and I will not have you treat her like a beggar at the door. Go downstairs and leave your mother to someone who knows what she's doing.'

'Carlos——' She made a brief attempt to argue, but some dark expression in the blue eyes decided her against it and she turned and left, glittering her hatred at Melodie as she passed her.

It was amazing, Melodie thought, when he left her alone with her patient, how amenable these apparently strong-willed women were, and she wondered vaguely if it had something to do with upbringing.

She found Mrs. Santas' temperature and pulse almost normal, although the pulse was still slightly fast, which was only to be expected when she was so obviously suppressing a pretty violent temper. Having examined her, however cursorily, Melodie was no longer puzzled by Keith's manner and his hesitation about bringing over the doctor. It was pretty obvious that the fainting fit had been brought about by nothing more or less than sheer bad temper, and she wondered what sort of a violent quarrel had brought on such fury.

She gave her verdict that there was nothing to worry about and the woman seemed to understand, nodding graciously, as if it was no more than she expected. 'I am obliged to you,' she told her in haughty and stilted English.

'I should stay and rest here for a while nevertheless,'

Melodie advised, and the dark eyes looked at her coldly.

'*Buenas noches,* Señorita Neil,' she said, and Melodie took it as a dismissal.

There was no sign of Maria when she came out of the bedroom, so she took it that the girl had done as she was told and gone downstairs, but Keith Scott was still waiting for her on the landing, and he smiled ruefully.

'I'm afraid I brought you out on a wild-goose chase, Melodie. I'm sorry.'

She shook her head. 'It's best if you have any doubts at all,' she told him as they walked down the stairs together. The very English atmosphere of the house surprised her rather, for no one would have suspected that the present owner was any less of a native Yorkshireman than the previous one had been, except perhaps that there were touches of luxury that were not usually found in English farmhouses.

She paused when they reached the hall and looked up at him curiously. 'I—I would have said that faint was due to some form of hysteria,' she told him, choosing her words with great care. 'It's evident Mrs. Santas has been under some emotional stress and that may have induced it.'

'I thought it might be something like that,' he said, apparently quite unperturbed about it, but not prepared to enlighten her further. 'But thank you for coming, Melodie.' He smiled wryly as he went off across the hall. 'I'll let Maria know that everything's O.K., then I'll take you home.'

'Oh, please don't bother,' she protested, 'it's stopped raining and I don't mind walking in the least.'

'You'll do no such thing,' he argued, with as much

firmness as he had shown when ordering Maria downstairs.

He did not wait for her to argue or pass an opinion, but went on to inform Maria that there was nothing to worry about, leaving Melodie in the hall. He was gone for only a few moments and when he rejoined her he took her arm and led her to the door, while she clutched at her purse in her pocket tightly.

'You're quite the most bossy man I've ever encountered,' she informed him, and he looked down at her, rather startled, she thought.

'Bossy?' He raised a brow and smiled his doubt as he saw her into the car. 'Surely not?'

'Surely you are,' Melodie insisted. 'Look at the way you—you *ordered* that poor girl out of the room!'

He grinned, tucking his long legs under the steering wheel. 'But she went, didn't she?' he said. 'It saves an awful lot of trouble.'

'For you, maybe,' she retorted. 'Quite frankly,' she added, as they drove off, 'I'm rather surprised at Miss Santas standing for it.'

He laughed and she saw from the glitter in his eyes that he was well pleased with things as they were. 'Maria's used to being told what to do,' he said. 'And she knows I have the whip hand.'

'I wouldn't put that past you, either,' Melodie retorted. 'As I said, you're bossy.'

'So are you,' he informed her surprisingly. 'Look how you laid down the law to me about my sheep straying, *and* when it was your fault too.'

'My——'

A brief but telling glance over his shoulder dared her to deny it and she allowed him to get away with it for the moment. 'Now don't argue the point,' he told her, before she could go any further. 'Your grandfather admitted it was your fault for not telling him about it.'

'A typical underhand trick,' Melodie objected, slipping down in her seat and refusing to look at him. 'Fancy trying to turn Grampy against me!'

'I wasn't trying to do anything of the sort,' he denied with a grin. 'It wouldn't do me any good to try anyway—he adores you.'

'He *likes* you,' she told him, nose in the air, 'but there's no accounting for taste.' She flicked him a look that was both curious and a little annoyed. 'I knew he'd would,' she added, 'at least I had a nasty feeling he'd like you.'

He cocked a brow at her, the smile in evidence again, as if the admission amused him. 'Is that why you didn't want us to meet?' he asked.

'No, of course it wasn't.'

He laughed, recognising a half-truth when he heard it. 'I don't believe you.' He flicked her a curious look, his expression more serious, as if he really wanted to know the answer. 'Does he like Jed Martin?'

Melodie frowned. Somehow she had expected him to bring up the subject of Jed again, but she was not prepared to discuss him or her grandfather's reaction to him, something she was still uncertain of. 'I don't see that that need bother you, Mr. Scott,' she said.

'It doesn't especially,' he confessed blandly, 'but it would be a bit awkward for you if the old man took a dislike to your intended, wouldn't it?'

'It makes no difference either way,' she told him. 'Grampy's not marrying Jed, I am.'

'Oh yes, of course.' She glanced at him suspiciously when he laughed softly to himself. 'It's official now, isn't it?'

'It is,' she agreed, 'but I don't see why you find it so funny.'

'No?' He grinned at her over his shoulder as they slowed down to turn into the drive at Millway. 'It just seemed to me from that little episode just before we left that your Jed's pretty bossy too, *amada*, and the old man isn't exactly meek and mild, is he? You're going to have your hands full with three of us to manage.'

She got out of the car, fumbling in her purse for her key and almost dropping it in her haste. 'You,' she told him as a parting shot, 'don't come into it, Mr. Scott.'

It was typical, she thought, as he drove away with an airy wave, that he should find that funny enough to laugh over.

CHAPTER FIVE

MELODIE stared at the contents of her purse in dismay, unable and unwilling to believe her eyes. It was two days since Jed had given her the ring and she remembered perfectly well putting it in her purse wrapped in a piece of paper. Now there was no sign of it.

Her mind raced frantically over her doings of the last couple of days, but nowhere in the chaos of thought could she recall a moment when she could have lost it. She had put it away safely, as she thought, when she went with Keith Scott over to Crowe's, and she had not taken it out since.

Jed had asked her if she had it safe and she had assured him that she had, and yet now, when he had rung to say that he was going into Cydale and wanted to take the ring with him to have it made smaller, she could not find it. How on earth, she wondered, was she going to tell him she had lost it? He had told her that he would be over for it in about an hour, and an hour seemed such a little time in which to search, especially since she had no idea where to start looking.

She confided in her grandfather, but with not much hope that he would produce a solution, and the old man shook his head when she asked him. 'I can't imagine where you could have lost it, love,' he told her. 'It's not long since you had it, so it can't be far away, can it? Have you been shopping at all?'

Melodie thought hard. 'Yes,' she remembered at last. 'I went into the village yesterday, but I wasn't gone long and I couldn't have——' She shrugged despairingly. 'I suppose I could,' she admitted ruefully.

'You can't remember if the ring was in your purse when you came back?'

She shook her head hopelessly. 'I just can't, Grampy. There's so many bits and pieces in my purse and the ring didn't take up much room, even wrapped up. I simply didn't notice if it was there or not.'

He looked at her, a little slyly, she thought. 'Your feller isn't going to take very kindly to the idea when he knows about it, is he?' he asked, and Melodie shook her head.

'I know that, Grampy, that's why I feel worse in a way than if it was a new one, although that'd be bad enough, goodness knows. Jed sets great store by that ring, it's—well, it's a sort of heirloom.'

The old man raised a curious brow. 'An heirloom?'

'Yes, it—it belonged to an aunt, she left it to him in her will. It's a very good one.'

'Aye, I noticed that,' he remarked, but did not enlarge on his meaning, although Melodie thought she followed the implication only too well, but refrained from saying so. 'Well, lass, the best thing would be to go back to when you had it last. You say you had it when you went over to Crowe's with Keith Scott, so presumably you had it when you came home, unless of course you lost it over there somewhere.'

'I don't see how I could have done,' she said. 'But it's possible, I suppose.'

'Then I suggest you start at the beginning, as it were,' her grandfather said. 'Walk over to Crowe's and see if they found it anywhere.'

'Oh, I can't do that,' Melodie objected, and the old man lifted his brows, his sunken face sharp with query.

'Why not?' he demanded.

'Because——' She shrugged impatiently. 'Oh, because he'd laugh at me for losing it so soon and then I should get furious with him.'

The old man smiled wryly. 'Isn't that better than Jed getting furious with you for losing it?' he asked. 'Go on, lass, Keith Scott won't eat you, and it's possible you did drop it over there somewhere and didn't notice it.'

'I suppose so.' She pulled a face over the prospect of visiting Crowe's again. 'I'd better go over there now and see if I can find it before Jed comes.'

He reached out for one of her hands and squeezed it gently. 'Don't let it worry you too much, lass, it's bound to turn up eventually and you couldn't help losing it.'

'Jed won't see it that way,' she told him gloomily. 'I don't know how I'm going to tell him.'

'Best take the bull by the horns and tell him straight

out if it doesn't turn up before he comes for it,' he grandfather advised, 'and worrying about it won't help, love.' He patted her hand. 'You run along and see if they've seen anything of it at Crowe's.'

'But surely if they had,' Melodie objected, 'Keith would have let me know. He saw the ring when I took it off and put it in my purse, because he spoke about it, and he'd almost certainly recognise it again.'

Her grandfather smiled knowingly. 'Maybe he did and he's letting you sweat for a while,' he suggested.

'If he is,' Melodie threatened darkly, 'I'll do something—something drastic to him, Grampy, I swear it!'

The thing Melodie found most off-putting about visiting Crowe's again was the possibility of meeting either Maria or her mother, and she was in two minds whether to turn back before she was half-way along the narrow road between Millway and Crowe's.

If only she had thought of it before she left, it would have been just as easy to telephone and ask if the ring had been found. It was thanks to her grandfather's insistence on her coming that she was now on her way over with a horrible tight sensation in the pit of her stomach that grew worse as she walked up the drive to the house.

A knock brought no reply and she had only just discovered a newly installed bell-push when she was hailed from somewhere behind and turned to see Keith looking at her, his brows almost disappeared into his hair in an expression of exaggerated surprise.

'Hel*lo*!' he said. 'To what do I owe this honour?'

She almost changed her mind again when she thought how he would receive the news, more reluctant than ever to tell him, now that it came to it. 'I— I'm sorry to bother you, Mr. Scott,' she said hesitantly.

'The only thing that bothers me,' he informed her solemnly, before she could tell him why she was there, 'is the fact that you so stubbornly and persistently refuse to call me Keith.'

'Please—I'm serious.'

'So am I,' he assured her. He mounted the one step to the front door and opened it, standing back to allow her to precede him, raising a brow in comment when she hesitated. 'Don't be frightened to enter the lion's den,' he told her, 'Mrs. Santas is here and Maria's out riding.'

'I don't even know if you can help me,' she said as she went into the hall and turned to face him.

'Oh, I'm sure I can.' He closed the door behind them with what sounded to Melodie like a rather ominous bang. 'But don't stand out here, come through into the sitting-room.'

'No, please, I can't stay very long and I must find— you see,' she explained. 'I've—well, I'm rather desperate in a way, and Grampy suggested I came here and asked if you could help, first.'

She looked very appealing and rather vulnerable standing there in the hall with her red head no higher than the breast pocket of his shirt, uncertain of herself and of his reaction. He looked down at her for a moment, his eyes more darkly blue in the dimness of the hall, then he reached out and put his hands on her arms, his fingers strong as they held her almost tight enough to hurt.

'Ask me anything you like, Melodie,' he said softly. 'I'll help if I possibly can, you know that.'

'It's—it's the ring. My ring,' she said.

'Your engagement ring?'

She nodded. 'I've lost it.'

'Oh-h!' She thought he looked relieved and wondered why else he thought she would have come to him. He shook his head and tut-tutted at her, his eyes showing more of their usual expression as they considered the idea. 'What will your Jed say about that?'

'It's not funny,' she told him reproachfully, shaking free of his hands, 'and I'm hoping I can find the wretch —the ring before he asks for it.'

'Oh?' He looked at her curiously. 'Is he likely to ask for it? Not already, surely?'

'What do you mean?'

'Well, asking for his ring back,' he explained. 'Have you come to the parting of the ways after so short a time? You haven't much staying power, have you?'

Melodie flushed, realising his meaning at last. 'You don't have to be so clever at my expense, Mr. Scott,' she told him. 'The ring's too big for me and I have to have it made smaller. Jed's going into Cydale, so he wanted to take it with him to the jeweller's. It was when he rang me to say he'd be collecting it that I realised I'd lost it.'

'It must have been a nasty shock,' he sympathised. 'When did you see it last?'

'When I put it in my purse on Sunday evening. You saw me do it.'

'Indeed I did,' he agreed. 'But don't tell me you haven't seen it since?'

She looked at him curiously, puzzled by his tone. 'No, I haven't.'

He smiled. 'Then you must be a very rare species, Melodie Neil. Not that I don't say you're not,' he added with a suggestion of a laugh.

'I don't see——' Melodie began.

'Most women I know would have had that ring out

91

every five minutes,' he explained. 'Trying it on and admiring it, but not you. Oh dear me no, you put it in your purse and promptly forget about it.'

'It wasn't that I forgot about it,' she protested, only vaguely wondering why she was bothering to explain to him. 'It's just that I'm not very fond of jewellery, and I thought it was quite safe where I put it.'

'That I can believe,' he grinned. 'You're nothing like the conventional starry-eyed bride-to-be, are you?'

She shook her head, refusing to be drawn into one of their interminable arguments. 'Have you seen the ring?' she asked. 'Could I have lost it here? Grampy suggested that I retraced my steps from the last time I remembered having it. It's so annoying,' she complained unthinkingly, 'why did he have to spring it on me so suddenly?'

He laughed as she should have expected. 'Very inconsiderate of him,' he remarked dryly. 'He should have guessed you'd lose it and been discreet enough not to ask about it.'

'Oh, don't be so clever,' Melodie wailed plaintively. 'It *must* be somewhere. In your car, perhaps?'

'We'll look,' he agreed, but a thorough search produced no ring and the housekeeper declared that it had not been lost in the house or she would have found it.

Melodie was near to tears of frustration when she left the farm, refusing Keith's offer to run her home as time was so short. 'I'll have enough to explain with the ring being lost,' she told him, 'without him seeing me with you as well.'

'Oh, I see.' He arched a brow and smiled as if the idea of Jed being jealous of him was not only amusing but quite understandable.

'Oh no, you don't,' Melodie retorted. 'It's just that he thinks——' She stopped herself in time from saying that Jed firmly believed Keith was annoying her with his attentions. She couldn't have borne the derisive laughter that would have invoked. 'Never mind,' she finished lamely. 'Thank you for helping me look for the ring, I'd better get back now and be there when Jed arrives.'

'Face the music?' he suggested sympathetically.

'Explain as best I can if I can't find it in the next half hour.'

She had not found it in the next half hour, and to make matters worse, Jed arrived earlier that he had said he would. She opened the door to him with her heart somewhere in the region of her soles and looked at him with such an expression of woe that his first reaction was to look across at the sitting-room where her grandfather was.

'Melly, what's wrong?'

She shook her head. 'It's not Grampy, Jed. I—I don't quite know how to tell you.'

'Tell me what, for heaven's sake?'

'It's the—my ring, Jed.' He knew, she thought wildly when she saw the slow frown gathering on his brow, he knew already. 'I—I think I've lost it.'

'You *think* you've lost it?' He was apparently as slow to anger as he was to everything else and, at the moment, she thanked heaven for it. 'Good grief, Melly, don't you know?'

'I—I yes, I know. I *have* lost it.' She faced the fact reluctantly and felt horribly close to tears, uncertain whether grief or self-pity caused them. 'I could cry,' she said dolefully.

'That'll do no good,' Jed told her bluntly, and not at

all sympathetically. 'Where did you have it last?'

Here we go again, Melodie thought morosely, and gave the same old answer. 'I had it here on Sunday, when I put it in my purse.'

'And you haven't looked at it since?' His reaction was much the same as Keith Scott's had been, except that he was definitely not amused about it.

'No.'

'So it could be anywhere?'

'Not anywhere,' Melodie denied. 'I've only been out twice since Sunday. Monday I met you in the spinney and I didn't have my purse with me then, and yesterday I went into the village.'

'Didn't you——' He had no time to complete the inevitable question before the door-knocker rat-tatted urgently and interrupted him.

Melodie started nervously and a second later felt a flicker of hope when she recognised the tall figure outlined against the pebble glass in the upper panel of the door. She briefly noted Jed's frown as she went to open the door and wondered if she was being too idiotically optimistic.

Before the door was open more than a couple of inches, a large hand appeared round the edge of it with the ring held between thumb and forefinger. '*Eureka* is the word, I believe,' Keith said, his grin conveying his pleasure at having surprised her.

She took the ring from him, shaking her head slowly, and wishing, rather unreasonably in the circumstances, that he had arrived five minutes earlier. 'I can't believe it,' she said, unsure whether to laugh or cry in her relief.

He lowered his voice, although it was impossible for Jed not to overhear. 'I thought I might have been in the nick of time,' he told her, his meaning obvious. He would have been in time too, Melodie thought wryly, if Jed had not arrived earlier than he'd said, and she flicked an anxious glance over her shoulder.

'I'm very grateful,' she said. 'Thank you, Keith.'

The use of his name seemed to please him inordinately and his smile was dazzling. 'It was worth it,' he claimed. 'And I'm glad I had my brainwave.'

'Won't you come in?' She opened the door wider and stood back, but he shook his head.

'No, thanks, Melodie, I've a call to make, but I had to follow my hunch, and it was right, you see.'

'But where on earth did you find it?' she asked, and he laughed, jerking a thumb over his left shoulder at the huge berberis growing against the house.

'Right on your doorstep,' he told her, and grinned broadly at her expression. 'I remembered that on Sunday when I brought you home you were so busy glaring at me that you fumbled for your key and nearly dropped your purse.' He shrugged and spread his hands, looking unbelievably foreign even with the sunny English landscape behind him. 'It was a long shot,' he admitted, 'but it didn't take long to find it.'

Melodie looked at him curiously. 'But wouldn't it have been much easier to have rung me and suggested that *I* looked under there?' she suggested. 'Instead of taking all the trouble to come over and look yourself.'

'I could have,' he agreed, 'but I'd have looked a bit of an idiot if it hadn't been there, and if you'd already thought of it and looked for yourself you'd have been very scathing because I hadn't given you credit for having enough sense to look, hence my Sherlock Holmes act and the *fait accompli*.'

'Well, I'm very grateful,' she said, smiling although she knew Jed was liking it less and less. 'Thank you, Keith.'

For a moment she thought he was going to kiss her hand, but instead he merely held it for a brief moment in what was more or less a handshake, his black head bowed over it. 'I believe in spoiling beautiful women,' he informed her solemnly, his voice outrageously seductive and low and the blue eyes glittering devilment as if he knew quite well the effect he was having on Jed.

'Well, thanks for taking the trouble,' Jed told him, taking a hand at last. 'We're very grateful, Scott.' It was a statement meant to put the caller firmly in his place, but Melodie doubted very much if it had the desired effect. Jed took the ring from her and carefully put it into the box he had taken from his pocket. 'I'd better have that, Melly, while it's still safe. When it's been made smaller and you're wearing it all the time you won't forget it so easily.'

It was, Melodie realised, not only a reproach for her for losing the ring, but also a way of reminding Keith of the significance of it, and she guessed what effect that would have on his irrepressible sense of humour.

'Don't have it made too tight a fit,' he told Jed, with every appearance of being serious, and Jed frowned at him curiously.

'No?'

'No,' he echoed. 'Women have a habit of changing their minds, you know.' He turned, waving a casual hand over one shoulder as he walked out to his car. ''Bye!'

It was a relief, Melodie had to admit, not to have the

responsibility of the ring on her conscience, especially as she had proved to be such a careless guardian. Jed had really been very good about it in the circumstances, in fact she thought he had been less disturbed by its loss than by Keith Scott recovering it.

The weather having picked up again, she wondered if she dared suggest to Jed that she take Michael for a picnic one afternoon. Picnics had been one of her greatest pleasures when she was small and staying at Millway. Her grandmother would bake some of her delicious cakes and pasties and they would take their tea down to the big lake which seemed unbelievably huge to a small girl. Surely, she thought, the pleasure of children could not have changed in so short a time.

Michael was nearly five, a small, solemn boy very much like his father. His mother had been dead almost three years now and the effect of his grandmother's rather overpowering personality was beginning to show itself in his quiet manner and oddly grown-up ways. Melodie had met him several times and, as far as she could tell, he liked her well enough, so she saw no reason why she shouldn't be entrusted with him for an hour or two, although his grandmother would probably produce several good reasons why she shouldn't. Mrs. Martin senior was less than enthusiastic about her son's relationship with her and it would, Melodie thought, prove to be the main obstacle in their plans.

Jed's permission obtained, Melodie baked parkin and a fruit cake, as her grandmother had done, and added some thickly buttered sandwiches for good measure. With lemonade and tea, they should be well supplied for a couple of hours in the open air.

The lake she remembered so well was no longer part of Millway, but she had already decided that she

97

would chance being discovered and take Michael there. The decision, she admitted, was as much to indulge her own nostalgia as for Michael's benefit, but the lake was an ideal spot.

The meadow grass smelled sweet and peppery in the warm sun, and the breeze had the first hint of autumn in it as it blew in off the moors. They went over the stones that crossed the stream and through a gate that admitted them to Keith Scott's property and the cool deep lake.

The peace of the place was almost unbelievable and even the grazing sheep in the next field seemed miles away. Michael, in the way of most small boys, was ready for his tea almost at once and he watched eagerly as Melodie unpacked their picnic basket. The edge of the lake rose slightly before it dropped down to the water and the sun reflected on the surface like a thousand little mirrors where the breeze ruffled it. Nothing, it seemed, could disturb the tranquillity of their picnic.

Michael set about his tea with a will and eagerly pointed out various things that caught his eye, including something that sounded like 'fishing', but it was rather muffled by a large sandwich and Melodie merely smiled without turning round to see what it was had attracted him.

It was several seconds later, as she was bent over the basket taking out more sandwiches, that two things happened at once, both so startlingly unexpected that she let out a squeak of surprise. There was a sort of plopping noise in the water just behind her and a second later she was splashed with enough of the lake's contents to soak her cotton dress through.

It flashed through her mind as she instinctively brushed her wet dress that Michael's 'fishing' must have been 'swimming' and the swimmer had landed inconveniently close to their picnic.

Michael was already on his feet, a half-eaten sandwich clutched in his hands, when Melodie recovered sufficiently to turn round, and the first thing she saw was what appeared to be some huge creature that stood right beside her dripping water all over the clean white cloth and the sandwiches spread on it. It was only when he smiled that she realised it was their unknowing host.

In all fairness, he did step back as soon as he realised the damage he was doing, and by then Melodie was on her feet, more concerned at the moment with her own soaking that with the damage their picnic had suffered. 'I might have known it was you,' she complained. 'Nobody's *ever* swum in that lake before. I should have known *you* would!'

He looked quite unperturbed by her annoyance, but smiled. 'It *is* my lake,' he reminded her, 'and it's rather a shame not to use it when it's here.'

She flushed at being reminded, however good-naturedly, that she and Michael were the intruders, and realised that by coming here she had played right into his hands if he felt inclined towards revenge for the number of times she had told him about trespassing.

'All right, it's your lake,' she allowed. 'Now I suppose you're going to have your revenge.'

He looked at her for several seconds until she felt she would have liked nothing better than to sink through the ground. He looked incredibly tall and more than usually dark-skinned in the brief swimming trunks he wore, and she could do nothing about the momentary skip her pulse gave at the sight of him. His thick black hair he swept back with the fingers of both hands, and in that stance he might have been some bronzed pagan god, she thought dizzily, as he stood there gleamingly wet in the warm sun.

'I'm sorry I splashed,' he told her at last quietly, and with a glimmer of amusement in his eyes, 'but I didn't expect to find you here, or anyone else for that matter.'

'Well, now you've ruined the sandwiches and soaked me to the skin, I hope you consider you've made your protest,' Melodie told him, and he laughed.

'Do you think I was making a protest?' he asked. 'Now why would I do that?'

'Tit for tat?' she suggested, and he laughed again, doing the inevitable thing to her pulse.

'Somewhere,' he said, looking along the bank, 'I've left a—ah! There it is.' He strode off to a spot some four or five yards away and returned carrying a big towel, rubbing his arms and body vigorously with it, while Michael and Melodie stayed in silence, one curious and the other distinctly uneasy. 'Now,' he said, when the operation was completed to his satisfaction, 'what makes you think I was making a protest?'

'I presumed you were,' Melodie said. 'Otherwise why smother me and our tea with water?'

He sat himself down on the grass on the other side of the basket and looked as if he was prepared to stay there and dry in the sun. 'Actually,' he confessed with a grin, 'I misjudged my distance, I should have come out just up there where my towel was; my clothes are there somewhere too.'

'Oh, I see. I didn't notice them.'

'Oh, it's all right,' he assured her solemnly, 'I won't offend your maidenly modesty by changing in full view.'

'Must you be so——' She cast a glance at Michael as she sat down again, wondering how much of the incident he would relay to his father, and also what significance Jed would see in it.

Keith grinned, looking at the boy. 'I don't think I know your young man, do I?'

'I'm Michael.' Obviously curiosity was uppermost in Michael's mind and he proffered a small hand which was engulfed in a large one and shaken solemnly, while he watched the newcomer with curious eyes.

'Michael is Jed's son,' Melodie explained. 'Michael, this is Mr. Scott.'

Michael took a moment to absorb the information, then he nodded knowingly. 'My dad knows you,' he declared.

'He does,' Keith admitted. 'And I know him.'

'You're a—a funnener.'

It was obvious what he was attempting to convey, and Melodie felt her own cheeks colour with embarrassment. Little pitchers have big ears, she thought ruefully, and obviously at some time or other, he had heard his father refer to Keith as a foreigner. It was pointless to expect Keith not to realise it too, and she did her best to show him that she was not involved in the incident.

'Michael!' she scolded the boy. 'That's not a nice thing to say.'

'Especially when you're having tea in my meadow,' Keith told him, only his eyes betraying the laughter that took it all in good part.

Michael frowned, in startling imitation of his father. '*Aren't* you a funnener?' he asked.

'Michael——' She would have remonstrated further, but a large and imperious hand waved her to

101

silence.

'To the English everybody's a foreigner, Michael,' he told the boy. 'I don't mind in a way, although it's not considered very polite to say it aloud.'

Michael absorbed that for a few moments in silence, evidently decided it was acceptable, and nodded.

'O.K.,' he agreed.

'I *am* sorry about trespassing on your land,' Melodie confessed, and wondered if he would understand if she told him her reasons. 'I——you see, I used to come here with my grannie for picnics, when I was little, and I——' She shrugged, half ashamed of being so nostalgic. 'I just thought I'd like to come again.' She looked at him, unconsciously appealing. 'That's my only excuse.'

'Why do you need an excuse?' he asked softly. 'It's a quite understandable feeling, the desire to visit old haunts.' He smiled, his eyes warm with understanding, so that she felt ridiculously like crying for some reason or other. 'Very sentimental but quite understandable,' he said, 'and at least it shows me that you don't look on me as quite the ogre you say you do.'

'I do no such thing!' she protested, then remembered again that Michael was there, and very much interested in everything that was going on, whether he understood it or not. 'I——I don't usually stray.' She looked up at the blue eyes watching her with a curious kind of intensity, and smiled. 'I'm not as bad as your sheep.'

'And so much more beautiful,' he told her softly, so that she bit her lip and hastily gave her attention to the picnic basket.

'Do we pack up and go right now?' she asked. 'Or can we stay and finish our tea first?'

'You can stay as long as you like,' he said. 'On one condition.'

She looked up again hastily, a small frown between her brows. 'Oh?'

'Yes, oh! That you let me stay and join you.'

She blinked her surprise for a moment, seeing Michael's added interest at the prospect. 'Stay by all means,' she told him. 'It's your land after all, I can scarcely order you off, can I?'

'But you *could* ask me nicely to stay,' he pointed out. 'Instead of accepting me on sufferance.'

Melodie smiled at the air of injured innocence he adopted, and nodded. 'Then please stay and have tea with us,' she told him. 'If you don't mind soggy sandwiches, that is.'

'Soggy or not, I'd love to stay,' he grinned. 'Now be a good girl and turn your back on that spot along there for a few minutes while I make myself more presentable, will you.'

It was an amazingly short time before he rejoined them and he looked as hungry as Michael had done, tucking into the sandwiches regardless of their rather limp state, and using the top of the flask to drink his tea from, demanding a piece of parkin when he had finished them.

'It's the least you can do in the circumstances,' he told her with a grin, and Melodie pulled a face.

'I'm not going to be allowed to forget this in a hurry, am I?' she asked as she handed him a piece of parkin on a paper plate.

'Well, you have rather asked for it, you must admit,' he told her. 'All the times you've evicted my poor old woollies from your precious acres, and telling me I had no right to ride across there, not to mention telling

Maria where she got off.'

'And revenge is sweet,' Melodie guessed wryly.

'Sweet and, in this instance, very tasty,' he agreed as another large bite of parkin disappeared.

If she had not met his eyes at that moment, she could at least have maintained the dignity of silence, but the brief eye-to-eye encounter was completely demoralising and she burst into laughter, while Michael looked at her with much the same expression as his father might have worn.

'You're even more beautiful when you laugh,' Keith told her, and it was only with difficulty that she managed to move back hastily before he touched her hand.

Her fingers were trembling in the most absurd way as she struggled with the lid of the cake box and she could actually hear the beat of her own heart. Nobody, she thought wildly, had ever had such a disturbing effect on her and it was high time she learned to overcome the sensation he always aroused.

The blue eyes watched her as she attended to Michael's wants, and she was aware of their scrutiny even though she refused to look at him. 'I like fruit cake too,' he told her. 'Don't I get some?'

He held out his plate and the expression on his face deceived her for a moment into thinking he was acting the little boy in competition with Michael, but then she saw the way his eyes were watching her, as if the soft curve of her mouth and throat fascinated him, and she realised the voice held as much mockery as persuasion.

It was as if some spell had been broken, only a second later, when Michael's flat little voice informed them that someone was coming. They both turned, reluctantly, to see the slim darkness of Maria Santas astride the black horse, galloping at breakneck speed across the meadow towards them.

Melodies' eyes widened and she flicked an anxious look at Keith. 'I don't think your—Miss Santas is going to like my being here,' she said. 'I'm sorry, Keith.'

'Why be sorry?' he asked, apparently unconcerned about the threatening storm. 'I own Crowe's, not Maria.'

'But——'

'But me no buts,' he told her firmly. 'You stay where you are and get on with your tea, leave Maria to me, and if you disgrace that red head of yours by backing down in front of Maria, I'll personally throw you in the lake, O.K.?'

'No, it's not——'

'Stay put and be quiet,' he said sternly as he got to his feet, and she glared at him balefully.

'You,' she said distinctly and with satisfaction, 'are bossy.'

There was no time for him to argue the point, for Diablo and his rider were upon them in an amazingly short time, the look on Maria's face when she saw the picnic was black as thunder. She reined in the horse dangerously close to where Melodie sat and looked down at her with glittering black eyes that suspected the worst.

'You go,' she told her, without even a glance at Keith to see what his feeling was in the matter. 'You go, now!'

He stood there with his feet apart, hands on his hips and ready for anything, Melodie thought, and only just suppressed a mad desire to giggle as she looked up at the two of them. The girl seemed in another world seated on the big black and Keith looked about ten feet tall standing right above Melodie seated on the ground.

He ran a hand through his still damp hair and smiled at Maria. 'Come and join the party,' he invited. 'I'm sure Melodie won't mind.'

Maria's long, slim hands clenched hard on the reins and her black eyes glowed like jet as she looked down at him, then she spoke, long and rapidly, in Spanish, her feelings obvious although the words were unintelligible.

He listened to her for a moment or two, then held up a large, forbidding hand and silenced her, his smile still in place but his mouth tighter at the corners. 'Either speak English or don't speak at all,' he told her. 'And don't translate what you've just said, Maria, or you'll wish you hadn't.'

'Carlos——' Again he held up a hand.

'If you want to join us, do so,' he told her, 'but don't argue, Maria.'

The proud, haughty face flushed with anger and she looked as if she would like nothing better than to strike Melodie with the crop she carried in one hand, instead she said something in Spanish that brought Keith's head up sharply and narrowed his eyes in a way that made him a stranger to Melodie.

His words were short and few and apparently very much to the point, for Maria's mouth tightened and her breathing was erratic enough to show as she held herself taut and straight in the saddle, then without another word, she dug her heels viciously hard into her mount and sent him racing off back the way he had come.

For a moment he watched her go and then, visibly making the effort to relax, he grinned down at Melodie and dropped on to the grass again. 'I'll have some more of that cake now,' he said.

She merely nodded in silence, while Michael, who had watched the proceedings with wide, interested eyes, looked from one to the other, his mouth full of fruit cake. 'That lady was cross,' he lisped through a shower of crumbs, and Melodie nodded absently. It was only as she watched Keith sitting there, so calmly munching his way through another piece of fruit cake, that she realised, she had no more thought of arguing with him than Maria had.

CHAPTER SIX

MELODIE found explaining their somewhat eventful picnic to Jed rather more difficult than she had anticipated, thanks mainly to Michael having already given his father his own version and apparently leaving out none of the details besides adding a few of his own.

When she met him the following afternoon as usual, she found him more garrulous on the subject than she had ever known him to be about anything. His homely face wore a frown that she realised would not be easy to dismiss, and she wondered just how exaggerated Michael's version had been.

'I don't understand why you had to go over there in the first place,' he told her. 'You know trespass is a touchy subject between you and Scott, Melly. What made you go?'

'Oh, I don't know, I just felt a bit nostalgic, I suppose,' she explained. 'I used to go to the lake for picnics when I was little.'

'Well, that's no reason for going there now, surely,' Jed argued. 'There are plenty of other places suitable for picnics.'

So much for his understanding her sentimental attachment for the place, Melodie thought ruefully. He evidently shared none of Keith Scott's feelings on the matter.

'I thought Michael would like it by the lake,' she said.

'Oh, he did,' Jed affirmed. 'He's done nothing but talk about it ever since he came home. He's near driven Mother mad with it.'

'Well, I'm glad he enjoyed it,' she said, imagining the old lady's annoyance at the idea of Michael enjoying himself without her company.

Jed's eyes narrowed as he looked at her, and she wondered apprehensively what she was to be charged with next. 'He says Scott had no clothes on,' he told her, and for a moment Melodie stared at him in startled surprise, then she burst into laughter and Jed's frown deepened. 'I don't see what's so funny about it,' he told her.

'I'm sorry, Jed,' she apologised when she was able.

'Well, I'm glad you find it amusing,' he told her stiffly, a faint flush on his weathered cheeks at what he took to be her mockery of him.

'But it is funny,' she insisted, 'because it's true—in a way.'

'True!' He looked so outraged that she almost laughed again. 'Melly, for God's sake what went on yesterday? I know this is a permissive age, but I won't have you——'

'He'd been swimming,' Melodie interrupted.

108

'In the——'

'In the usual garb men wear for swimming,' she said, a bit impatiently. 'Oh, Jed, can't you see? That's what struck me as so funny—in a way Michael was right, but it wasn't as bad as you obviously thought it was.' She looked at him from under her lashes. 'You didn't have much faith in *my* good sense, did you?'

'I only knew what Michael told me,' he said, with bad grace. 'I've never known anyone go swimming in that pond before. It's a sure sign he's a foreigner, he's as mad as a hatter.'

'I don't see why you should think that,' she objected, remembering Michael's embarrassing statement on the subject yesterday. 'It's very deep and it's quite clean, ideal for swimming if you're a strong swimmer.'

He looked at her sharply and she wondered, in one enlightening moment, why she had ever considered him placid and quiet. There were depths to Jed's character she had not even suspected, and he was far less slow and without emotion than she had realised.

'I thought you disliked Scott,' he said. 'It's the impression you always gave. Or has something happened to change your mind?'

'No, of course not!' She was aware that she was treading on dangerous ground when she started analysing her feelings towards Keith Scott, but she told herself nothing had really changed. He was still arrogant *and* conceited and she did not envy Maria Santas in the least being engaged to him—if indeed she was. But she lowered her eyes before the shrewd, rather disconcerting look in Jed's.

'That Spanish woman came and—saw you too,' he said, and Melodie was convinced that he had almost said 'caught you.'

109

'Maria Santas,' she nodded. 'Yes, she came up while Keith—while he was talking to us; riding as usual. She seems to spend all her time riding horses.'

'What did she have to say?'

Melodie smiled wryly. 'Apart from an initial order to me to get off what she evidently considers her land,' she told him, 'I haven't the remotest idea—it was all in Spanish and I gathered it was very rude.'

'What happened?'

She shrugged, as if he should have known the outcome without being told. 'She rode off like a lamb when he told her off,' she said. 'At least I suppose he was laying down the law, it sounded very much like it.'

Jed's rather humourless mouth crooked into a momentary smile as if the idea actually amused him. 'She has to mind her p's and q's, does she?'

'She seems to.'

He looked puzzled. 'I'm surprised she takes it from him, frankly. From what I've seen of her, she looks like a real handful, not the amenable type at all.'

'She's in love with him,' Melodie stated simply, and wondered after she'd said it whether it was love or some other equally strong emotion that made Maria Santas so jealous and so anxious to please the man she evidently considered was her property.

Jed shook his head, his hazel eyes acknowledging the vagaries of women. 'I suppose that accounts for a lot,' he said. 'Some folk go completely silly when they get to that stage.'

Melodie looked at him curiously as they walked through the spinney, studying the rather heavy features and short, square chin, wondering if his wanting to marry her had much to do with love as she had always thought of it. She had told him that she did not love

110

him in the usual way and he had seemed content with that, and she *was* very fond of him. He was kind and reliable, but she was increasingly aware of his lack of romance. They were walking along now, through the sun-dappled spinney with the bird-song soft and sweet all round them, but Jed did no more than hold her hand and she realised, with a start, she could almost count the times he had kissed her.

She stopped so suddenly that he turned and looked at her, his expression mildly curious. 'Something wrong?' he asked, and Melodie shook her head.

'Not really.' She faced him, her fair skin shadow-dappled with the sun through the trees, her green eyes wide and speculative as she studied him. 'Have you got to that stage, Jed?' she asked.

'Stage? What stage?' He had evidently quite forgotten his previous statement and Melodie, rather impatiently, reminded him of it.

'You said people in love go completely silly when they get to that stage,' she said. 'Have you got to the —the silly stage yet, Jed?'

He stared at her for a moment in silence, then frowned. 'I'm not the silly type,' he told her. 'At least I hope I'm not.'

'No. No, of course you're not.' What disappointment she felt betrayed itself in her voice and he put his hands to her arms and pulled her closer to him, realising at last that he was falling far short of her expectations.

'I'm sorry, Melly,' he said. 'I'm not much of a man for making a fuss, but you know how I feel about you, don't you?'

'I expect I do.' The frown deepened, becoming embarrassed, she recognised.

111

He looked down at her, frankly puzzled, and she could not help but remember the way Keith Scott had looked at her yesterday beside the lake. Of course he was probably a practised philanderer, and he certainly cared little for Maria Santas' feelings, whether or not he was engaged to her, but just for once she would have liked Jed to gaze at her mouth in the same, intense way that made her think she was about to be kissed.

'I've asked you to marry me,' he said.

Melodie smiled wryly. 'In actual fact you haven't,' she told him, and he blinked at her uncertainly.

'But I gave you the ring.'

Melodie shook her head, feeling rather mean for behaving as she was, but some niggling, capricious little imp of contrariness egged her on. 'You've never asked me to marry you, Jed, you've just taken it for granted. You asked Grampy, not me.'

'Oh, Melly, for goodness' sake,' he said shortly. 'I thought you were a practical girl. You don't need pretty speeches, do you?'

'Yes, I'd love pretty speeches,' Melodie declared, her chin in the air. 'And just for once, Jed, I'd like to hear you say *why* you want to marry me.'

He stood and gazed at her, obviously not quite believing what he heard, his round face slightly flushed as if the subject embarrassed him. 'What's come over you, Melly?' he asked at last. 'You seem—I don't know, different lately. You used not to bother about silly little things like that.' He looked at her earnestly, his hands firm on her arms. 'What's wrong, lass?'

Melodie sighed, seeing the futility of her brief bid for romance. 'Nothing, Jed. Nothing's wrong. I'm sorry if I worried you.'

'You didn't,' he admitted frankly. 'But I'm damned if I can make head or tail of you lately, I don't know what to think.'

'I'm no different from usual,' she said, and wondered how true it was. Once she had been quite content with Jed's plain, undemonstrative company, but lately she found herself getting impatient with him, wishing he would show a little more warmth and affection. Even if she did not actually love him as she had always thought of the word, she felt that with a little more encouragement from him she would come nearer to the ideal state. It was surely not too much to ask that he should kiss her occasionally and behave as if he loved her and wasn't just seeing her as a stepmother for his son.

'You're not worried about Michael, are you?' he asked, with startling insight into her thoughts. 'I mean, about how he'll take to the idea of us being married?'

'I have sometimes wondered if it'll work out as well as you seem to think,' she confessed, but did not say that she saw his mother and not his son as the main obstacle.

'But he likes you, you know that,' he insisted. 'He's said so, though of course you couldn't really take Mother's place.'

'His or yours?' Melodie asked, and immediately shook her head apologetically. 'No, of course I couldn't take anyone's place,' she said. 'I don't expect to.'

She would have turned then and continued with their walk, but the hands on her arms tightened suddenly and drew her against him, his mouth seeking hers in a kiss that surprised her with its warmth and feeling. 'Melly!' His face rested on the softness of her hair and his arms were tight around her. 'I *do* love you, Melly, even if I'm not very good at saying so.'

It was not very often that Melodie went very far afield, but occasionally she went into Cydale for an hour or two and browsed around the shops, then treated herself to a lunch in one of the smaller cafés before returning home. Cydale was not exactly a big city, but it was a fair-sized town and it offered far more distractions than the village did. She knew her grandfather would be in safe hands with Mrs. Bazeley, for the housekeeper was completely trustworthy and was, actually, very fond of the old man.

Melodie had never learned to drive and her visits to Cydale were one time when she wished she had, for although the bus service was quite good, it was a much longer journey than the same distance would have been in a car and thus made her time there much shorter.

She had very little shopping to do, but she always enjoyed a leisurely wander round the bigger shops after her tasks were done. She was strolling slowly along the main street admiring the goods in a big store window and thinking of finding some lunch when she felt a hand on her arm.

She spun round, quite startled by the unexpectedness of it, and found Keith Scott's deep blue eyes looking down at her, showing the inevitable amusement at having startled her. 'Daydreaming?' he asked.

'I was,' she confessed, 'but I don't expect to be accosted in the streets of Cydale.'

His gaze swept over her features, the cheeks slightly flushed and the eyes wide and shiny, and he smiled. 'You surprise me,' he said. 'I would have thought you'd have been accosted anywhere, even in no-nonsense Yorkshire.'

'There's as much nonsense in Yorkshire as anywhere else,' she informed him, doing nothing about the hand

114

that still lay rather possessively curled over her arm.

'Is there?' Black brows shot upwards in exaggerated surprise, as if she had said something outrageous and she looked around her uneasily. It was not often she saw anyone she knew, but one never knew and it would be difficult to hope that anyone would overlook Keith Scott.

'Are you shopping too?' she asked, and he nodded, recognising her uneasiness and amused by it as always.

'In a way, but I was about to have lunch before I collapse with hunger.' He cocked a brow at her. 'Where, may I ask, were you heading for when I brought you out of your daydream?'

She hesitated, suspecting what the possible outcome of her admission would be, but unwilling to lie about it. 'As a matter of fact,' she said, 'I was just thinking of finding some lunch too.'

He looked around them with exaggerated caution. 'Alone?' he asked, and she nodded.

'Alone.'

He tut-tutted, as if the idea scandalised him. 'There should be a law against beautiful women lunching alone,' he told her solemnly. 'Just think, anything could happen to you. You could be approached by the most undesirable characters and persuaded into heaven knows what sort of compromising position.' He shook his head slowly. 'No,' he said, 'I can't allow that to happen, you definitely can't lunch alone. Will you join me?'

Melodie suppressed an almost irresistible desire to laugh which she firmly subdued, for one thing because she was feeling rather self-conscious about the ring which she now wore on her left hand. 'I'm—I'm not sure it would be——'

115

'Discreet?' he enquired softly, and laughed. 'Oh, come on, Melodie, be a devil and risk the gossip.'

'It's not gossip I'm bothered about,' she informed him, her cheeks pink. 'It's the—the ethics of it.'

'I notice you're wearing *the* ring,' he said with a grin, 'but that doesn't stop you eating, does it?'

'No, but——'

'Then let's go, for heaven's sake, before we take root. I'm hungry.'

'So am I, but, Keith——'

'Come on!' He put a hand under her elbow and she had very little option but to go along with him, or else create a scene, and that was the last thing she wanted to do.

'Where are you taking me?' she asked, a bit breathless with trying to match his stride.

'The Weldon, do you know it?'

'I know of it,' she admitted. 'I've never been there, it's much too grand for the occasional modest lunch in town.'

He grinned down at her.' Poor little country mouse,' he jeered.

She kept pace with him as best she could for another few yards, then stopped short, automatically bringing him to a halt too, a look of enquiry on his face. 'Will you slow *down*?' she complained. 'I shan't have breath enough left to eat if you keep up this pace!'

He laughed, but obligingly slowed down. 'Shorty!' he taunted. 'I forgot you're pint-sized.'

'I'm a respectable five feet two,' Melodie retorted, glancing up at him. 'We can't all be beanpoles,' she added.

'Beanpoles? I'm a respectable six feet two. And I think I'll call you Vestas,' he added, grinning down at

116

her as he waited for the inevitable reaction.

Melodie looked at him suspiciously. 'You've called me practically everything else you can think of,' she said resignedly, 'but why Vestas?'

'Small, slender, red-headed and gives off sparks,' he countered swiftly. 'Can you think of a better one?'

'For a foreigner,' Melodie told him, 'you certainly make free with our language.'

'*My* language,' he told her quietly, and in such a tone of voice that she looked at him curiously.

'That's meant to be informative, isn't it?' she asked, and he smiled.

'Clever girl!'

She walked beside him up the steps to the restaurant, still frowning her curiosity. 'Keith, must you be so infuriating?'

He did not answer her but merely smiled and concentrated on catching the head waiter's eye. The Weldon was fairly new and quite the grandest place that Cydale had ever seen, but its keynote was quiet good taste rather than ostentation, and Melodie momentarily forgot her curiosity about her companion and looked around her with interest. Keith Scott was the kind of man that head waiters instinctively took notice of and they were soon seated at a table for two and the menu presented for their study.

'I suppose a lot of these people are here for the motor racing at Cyley Park,' she guessed, while they waited for their lunch to arrive. 'They look too grand to be local folks.'

'Ah-ah, Toffee-nose,' he reproved. 'We're local folks, don't forget.'

'Not strictly speaking,' she argued, 'and anyway I wasn't being snobbish. You can always tell out of town

117

people somehow.'

'How?'

She frowned over it for a moment. 'I don't know,' she confessed at last. 'You just can, that's all.' She looked at the dark expressive face opposite her and laughed. 'Nobody would take you for a local anyway,' she told him, 'no matter what you say.'

'You know,' Keith told her sternly, 'sometimes I suspect you're a racialist.'

'I'm nothing of the sort,' she objected. 'I don't care *what* people are or where they come from.'

He made no comment, much to her surprise, but looked unusually serious for several minutes before he spoke again, and then he did not look at her but at the fork he twirled with uncharacteristic restlessness between his long fingers.

'I *am* local folks, Melodie,' he said at last, as if he was anxious to impress her with the fact. 'Or at least I will be if all goes well. I've taken out naturalisation papers.'

'Keith!' She stared at him for a few seconds, almost ready to believe that he was teasing her again, but she knew from his expression and his manner that he wasn't. 'Aren't—aren't you ever going back to the Argentine again?' she asked.

'Oh yes, sometimes. Occasionally, as I do now, as I *have* to do now because I'm an alien, but——' He shrugged his broad shoulders and looked up at last, a hint of smile already in his eyes as if he regretted the moment of solemnity. 'I've spent so much time over here that I feel as if I belong, and I'd like to be able to stay for good, settle down here.'

'But Miss—Maria——' she began, and he looked at her steadily, shaking his head.

118

'What I decide has nothing to do with Maria,' he said quietly. 'On matters as important as this I make my own decisions regardless of other people's opinions.'

'Yes, of course.' Of course, she thought wryly, and that probably explained that quarrel that Maria Santas and her mother had had with him when Mrs. Santas had become so furious that she had fainted. They came from proud Spanish stock, that was obvious, and the idea of Maria being married to what would amount to a plain, honest Yorkshire farmer must have been quite a shock.

'You don't approve?' He sounded almost anxious, and she shook her head.

'No, no, I couldn't do other than approve,' she said. 'You like it here and you—you fit in very well.'

His laugh held a hint of mockery, but she could not help the smile it induced. 'God knows why anybody *wants* to stay in this potty little country,' he said, 'but it's much more home to me than anywhere else, and at least I don't have to anglicise my name.'

'Your great-great-grandfather would have been pleased, I expect,' she ventured, and he nodded.

'No doubt,' he agreed. The wine waiter having supplied their wants, he raised his glass to her. 'Shall we drink to the success of the venture?' he said, and she raised her own glass willingly.

'The best of luck, Keith,' she told him. 'I hope you get what you want.'

He smiled, his eyes watching her mouth again in that disturbing and intense way that made her lower her eyes hastily. 'I usually do,' he told her quietly, and she had no difficulty in believing him.

'Will you like being British?' she asked, and glanced

up to see him looking surprised.

'Like it? Of course I shall like it, you funny infant, or I shouldn't have taken the trouble to get myself naturalised.' The deep blue eyes looked at her quizzically. 'Now what was behind that question, I wonder?'

'I was only thinking,' Melodie explained, 'that it would be quite a bit different being a visiting—gentleman from the Argentine, and being—well, just another Englishman, if you'll forgive the phrase.'

'Isn't it possible to be an Englishman and still be a gentleman?' he asked, evidently finding the subject amusing.

'Oh, you know what I mean,' she retorted. 'There must be certain advantages to being a—a blue-eyed *señor*—especially with the women.'

The blue eyes in question gleamed wickedly and that disturbing laugh trickled along her spine once more. 'I suppose there are advantages in that direction,' he allowed. 'But what makes you think it interests me to that extent?'

'Oh, of course it does!' She could feel the warmth in her cheeks, but it was too late to go back now, and he could scarcely claim disinterest in the opposite sex after the way he had behaved towards her, and while he was supposed to be engaged to Maria Santas too.

'Of course it does,' he mocked. 'I admit I like beautiful women, Melodie, but you make me sound like the traditional Latin lover.' He laughed again as if the idea amused him immensely. 'It's a marvellous thought, I must admit.'

She looked at him thoughtfully, her heart fluttering rapidly under her ribs when he met and held her gaze. She had drunk very little wine as yet and it had certainly not had time to have any effect, and yet she felt

120

amazingly lightheaded and reckless.

'Jed,' she informed him solemnly, 'thinks you're no better than you ought to be.'

He laughed, taking her left hand in his and looking down at the ruby and diamond ring sparkling on the third finger. 'That's a quaint phrase,' he said softly, 'and considering what a fool Jed is, I don't think I care too much what he thinks of me.'

'Oh no! You shouldn't say that!' The harsh criticism of Jed jolted her back to earth, her conscience pricking her sharply so that she tried to pull back her hand, looking at him with huge, reproachful eyes when he held on to it. 'Jed's the kindest and most thoughtful man I've ever met,' she went on, determined to salve her conscience. 'He couldn't be kinder or—or more reliable.'

'I'm sure he couldn't,' he agreed quietly, still holding her hand, 'but I still say he's a fool. If you were mine *I'd* take good care that no other man took you out to lunch.'

'Well, I'm not——' She stopped in mid-sentence when someone stopped beside their table, a half-smile of recognition on his face.

It was a sharp, curious face and he flicked a narrow gaze from Keith to herself and back again before addressing himself to Keith. 'Keith Scott!' he said. 'It *is* Keith Scott, isn't it?'

If Keith remembered the man he did a very good job of concealing it, but he looked politely curious as he released Melodie's hand and nodded agreement. 'I'm Keith Scott,' he admitted. 'I'm afraid I don't——'

'Oh, I don't suppose you remember me, we only met once,' the man told him with a short laugh, his voice sounding embarrassingly loud even in the busy restaurant. 'There were about fifty of us there. Joe Ennells—*Sporting View*; I've seen you a lot more often than you've seen me, Mr. Scott. In the good old days, of course.'

'Ah, a sports-writer——' The fact seemed to explain it all to him, although Melodie, who admitted to an appalling ignorance in sports matters, was just as much in the dark as ever.

'I've covered your polo-playing exploits in a good many places,' the reporter told him. 'It's a great pity you gave it up, you were one of the best.' Sharp eyes glanced again at Melodie and he smiled. 'Still, some things don't change, eh?'

'That's right,' Keith agreed quietly, his attitude not exactly encouraging.

The man looked briefly discomfited, then he laughed again and shook his head. 'Ah well, I'll leave you to your lunch.' Another swift curious glance came Melodie's way before he raised a hand in casual salute and went off. 'Nice to have seen you again,' he called.

When he had gone Melodie had the strangest feeling that Keith was uneasy about something, but since it was no more than a vague instinct she said nothing. Her companion was quiet for a few minutes when they were alone again, then he smiled, pulling a face by way of apology.

'I'm sorry about that,' he said. 'I don't remember ever meeting the man, but obviously I have at some time or other.'

'In your misspent youth of long ago?' she queried, and laughed at the black-browed frown she incurred.

'Not so much misspent as over-spent,' he told her. 'And I'll thank you not to set my youth too far back in history, my girl.'

122

'You called me an infant just now,' she reminded him, 'so I took it you must be at least ninety, and from the funny look in that reporter's eye your youth *must* have been misspent.'

He smiled a slow, slightly crooked smile that glistened in his eyes. 'And so you're interested,' he guessed, and shook his head. 'I suppose it was misspent in a way,' he admitted. 'But I enjoyed it.'

'You were a polo-player?' It was easy to imagine him playing that fast, furious and at times dangerous game; no wonder he was such a good horseman.

He nodded. 'Quite a good one,' he said with a smile, 'hence the interest of our journalist friend.'

'You must have travelled around a lot.' There was an unconcealed hint of envy in her voice which he recognised with an understanding smile.

'It was a hectic life and a gay one,' he admitted, and added with a soft laugh, 'A very, very gay one at times.'

Melodie was intrigued and made no secret of it, resting her elbows on the table, looking at him over the rim of her glass. 'South American playboy polo-player,' she said with a smile. 'So my estimation of you as a— a Latin lover *wasn't* wrong after all?'

He laughed, taking one of her hands in his and briefly pressing his lips to the palm. 'You ask too many questions, *enamorada*.'

'You're speaking Spanish again,' Melodie pointed out, her voice as well as her hands feeling horribly unsteady. 'It's rude, at least you told Maria—Miss Santas it was.'

'And I told you I was exempt from the rules,' he reminded her. 'And just one little endearment,' he protested. 'You surely don't object to that, do you?'

She swallowed another sip of wine to try and steady

123

the uneasy throbbing in her temple. 'I don't think you should use endearments at all in the circumstances,' she told him, and he took her hand again as she put down her glass, looking thoughtfully at the ring she wore on it.

'In the circumstances,' he echoed softly. 'No, I suppose I shouldn't.' He raised her hand and kissed her fingers briefly before releasing it. '*Perdone, señorita.*'

'You're doing it again!'

'So I am.' His laugh made a mockery of her objections and he was watching her with a wicked look in those deep blue eyes that brought a flood of colour to her cheeks. He was, Melodie thought wildly, quite the most exasperating and the most disturbing man she had ever met, and thank heaven Jed wasn't there to see her reaction to him. He would never have understood her—she was not even sure that she understood herself.

CHAPTER SEVEN

JED was not at their usual meeting place the day following Melodie's visit to Cydale, but she was not too surprised, for sometimes he had other things to do and they had never made a definite arrangement. In fact it was only quite recently that the more or less daily meeting had become a regular thing.

It was much more of a surprise, however, when he came to the house—an occurrence which was quite soon explained. She had just settled her grandfather for a nap and Jed's arrival was not really welcome, for the old man would use any excuse not to be, as he termed it, treated like a baby and made to sleep during the day.

Hearing their voices in the hall he called out to them. Melodie made a face as she went in to him, followed hestitatingly by Jed. 'We can talk in the other room, Grampy,' she told him. 'You must get your sleep.'

'I don't want to sleep,' her grandfather declared, and spoke to Jed, still hovering in the doorway. 'You can come in here, Mr. Martin,' he told him. 'I'm not sleeping. Glad to have an excuse not to.'

'Grampy——'

'So I am,' the old man insisted. 'I'd much rather talk to somebody.'

Melodie sighed. 'All right, if you insist.'

'I do.'

'It was—well, a bit private what I had to say to Melly,' Jed told him, using his own version of her name for the first time in the old man's hearing, and her grandfather frowned over it.

'Melodie hasn't any secrets from me,' he informed Jed. 'Have you, lass?'

Melodie looked at Jed warily, suspecting for the first time the object of his visit. His attitude, plus his unusual action in coming to the house to see her, made her uneasy. Yesterday's lunch with Keith Scott still gave her a slightly guilty feeling when she thought about it, but how Jed could possibly have learned about it puzzled her.

It was possible that someone who knew them both had seen her with Keith, of course, but usually the type of person who would take great pleasure in telling Jed

125

about it would have been equally unable to resist speaking to her while she was with Keith, and letting her know she had been seen.

She looked at him for a moment before deciding. 'If you want to talk to me alone very particularly, Jed, we *can* go into the other room.' The unexpected and unaccustomed hardness in his eyes worried her. 'Is something wrong?' she asked quietly, and he looked at her steadily.

'I'd rather we talked alone, Melly.'

'Yes—yes, of course, if you'd rather.' She tucked the blanket in around the old man's knees more firmly, smiling absently as she did so. 'I'll take Jed in the back room, Grampy, you try and get some rest.'

Her grandfather's shrewd dark eyes looked at Jed speculatively and it looked as if he had made up his mind to have his say no matter if it was welcome or not. 'I suppose it's about that lunch with Keith Scott yesterday?' he said, and both Jed and Melodie looked at him in surprise. Melodie because she had thought him more tactful than to mention it, and Jed because he was obviously startled by his knowing about it.

'You know about that?' he asked, and the old man nodded.

'I told you, Melodie has no secrets from me.'

Jed's homely face looked worried and he seemed uncertain what to say or do next. 'I was very surprised, Melly. What made you do it?'

'Have lunch with him?' She wondered how best to answer. The truth was uncomplicated enough, but would he believe it? 'I was shopping,' she said. 'One of my occasional jaunts into Cydale, and I was just thinking of going to lunch when he came up and spoke to me.'

'He would!' Jed declared, and Melodie frowned impatiently.

'For heaven's sake, Jed, it was a perfectly normal thing to do if you see a neighbour in town,' she protested. 'Be reasonable about it. He said he was just going to have lunch and asked me if I'd join him.'

'And you said yes, of course.'

She disliked the suggestion of sarcasm. 'I said I wasn't sure if I should,' she retorted. 'But he seemed to think my—my reticence was highly amusing, and shanghaied me into the Weldon almost before I realised where I was going.'

'The Weldon?' He looked quite scandalised, and Melodie thought he was thinking of the prices at Cydale's latest restaurant. 'He *must* be made of money.'

'I don't think he's exactly poor,' she agreed quietly.

'And he wasn't averse to showing off either, I suppose,' he guessed.

'He didn't give the impression he was trying to show off,' Melodie denied, aware that her grandfather was supporting her, even if it was in silence. There was no disguising the look of satisfaction on his face.

'Well, all I can say,' Jed went on, not to be so easily persuaded, 'is that you should thank your lucky stars you're not engaged to *him*, Melly, like that Spanish girl is.'

'Maria Santas is Argentinian,' she corrected him, her temper rapidly gaining control.

'Whatever she is,' Jed retorted, 'she has my sympathy.'

'Because he took me to lunch?'

'Because he seems incapable of leaving you alone whenever he sees you,' Jed stated firmly. 'Don't pretend you haven't seen it, Melly. He takes every oppor-

127

tunity that offers itself to—to speak to you, or take you to lunch.'

'It was the first time he's taken me to lunch,' Melodie objected.

'Anyway, who can blame him, if he does like talking to a beautiful girl?' They both looked a little startled at the old man's interjection, having almost forgotten he was there. 'Melodie's a very lovely girl,' he went on when neither of them spoke. 'Any man would make the most of his chances in the circumstances.'

'But you're engaged to me,' Jed said, as if the argument had been hers.

'I know I am, but for heaven's sake, Jed, it doesn't mean I have to—to go into purdah!' She remembered suddenly that that had been Keith Scott's opinion and wished she had chosen some other metaphor. 'I had lunch with him, that's all, nothing to make such a fuss about surely.'

'Mother saw you.'

'Oh, I see.' She nodded understanding. 'I wondered who'd told you.'

'You wouldn't have said anything yourself, would you?' he challenged, and she wondered if she ever would have or not.

'As it turns out you can see why I hesitated to tell you,' Melodie retorted. 'You didn't give *me* a chance to tell you, you took your mother's word for it that I was deceiving you.'

'She was only thinking of me,' Jed insisted, as if he only now realised the mischief that had been caused. He looked down at his feet, embarrassed and uneasy, especially with the old man's shrewd gaze fixed on him so speculatively. 'Mother thought I—I might be upset by it.'

'And you were,' she said dryly, but he shook his head.

'More surprised than upset, Melly. I knew you wouldn't do anything really underhand.' Now that he had heard her explanation and, so Melodie considered, been put in his place, his hazel eyes looked anxious and rather appealing.

'But you came to lecture me on my sins just the same.'

'No, no, it wasn't that at all,' he objected. 'I was all for saying nothing about it, but——' He stopped so suddenly that it was obvious he had already said more that he meant to, and Melodie nodded understanding.

'But!' she echoed. 'I suppose your mother meant it for the best, Jed,' she told him, 'but need she have said anything at all if she thought it would upset you?'

'She—she thought I had a right to know,' he explained, sounding very apologetic, so that she felt rather sorry for him. 'She doesn't know you as well as I do, Melly.'

'No.' She bit her lip. 'I suppose that's why you didn't come to the spinney yesterday afternoon, isn't it?'

He nodded. 'I had to think first. You know how I dislike you having anything to do with Scott. I don't trust the man and I—well, I didn't want to see you too soon and, in the heat of the moment, say something I'd be sorry for afterwards.'

In the heat of the moment did not sound in the least like Jed, but she was discovering new sides to Jed every day. 'You could have trusted me,' she told him, and he nodded.

'I'm sorry, Melly.'

'Oh!' She took his arm and looked up into the stolid,

129

kindly and, at the moment, rather unhappy face. 'Oh, it doesn't matter, Jed. It was just a lunch, that's all, nothing to bother about, and if your mother had spoken to me when she saw me I'd have been quite unconcerned.' That wasn't quite the truth, she realised, but she had nothing really to reproach herself with.

He shook his head, a small frown between his brows. 'You know how it is,' he said. 'Mother's inclined to worry too much about me.'

'Naturally.'

'Maybe,' old James Neil suggested slyly, 'she'll have less to worry about when you're married again.'

'Oh—oh yes, I suppose so.' He looked a bit sheepish, Melodie thought, and wondered why.

'When are you going to name the day?' the old man asked blithely, and Melodie stared at him wide-eyed. He had never before shown any sign of wanting her to get married, in fact if anything he had been rather more the other way around, and she wondered why he had suddenly become so keen to hurry her into it.

Jed looked, if anything, even more taken aback than Melodie and he flicked her a brief uneasy glance before he answered. 'Well, there are things to be considered, Mr. Neil,' he said at last.

'Things?' the old man asked shortly. 'Or people?'

'Both—in a way.' He was rapidly getting out of his depth, Melodie thought, and she should help him along, but instead she merely waited to see what he would do.

'You mean me?' her grandfather asked bluntly, and Jed glanced at Melodie again.

'In a way, yes,' he admitted. 'I know Melodie means a lot to you, Mr. Neil, and you need careful nursing, she wouldn't want to entrust that to anyone else, I know.'

'Looking after a crotchety old man is no substitute for being married to a young one,' the old man told him shortly. 'But I don't see why it can't be worked out, if all the parties are agreed.'

'Grampy,' Melodie looked at him warily, 'what are you talking about?'

'Why, you marrying Jed, of course,' her grandfather said. 'If it's only me that's holding things up, then I'm prepared to sell up and move house, live at Jed's place with you two and his family. That way we can kill two birds with one stone.'

It was obvious from his expression that Jed had never considered the idea, and Melodie certainly hadn't, so that the suggestion was greeted initially with a rather uneasy silence.

'I—I hadn't thought of that,' Melodie said at last, glancing at Jed.

'I'm not sure it could be done, Mr. Neil,' Jed said slowly. 'I mean I'm not sure we could make a satisfactory arrangement.' He looked at Melodie apologetically, as if he was asking for her understanding at least. 'You see—well, it's Mother. The house is half hers and I can't just do as I like in it.'

'Oh well,' the old man said, apparently undismayed. 'We'll have to think of something else, that's all.'

'There's really no hurry, is there?' Melodie protested, looking at him reproachfully. 'Unless you're in such a hurry to see me married, Grampy.'

'*I'm* not,' her grandfather assured her. 'I just don't want to think I'm standing in the way of true love, that's all.'

'Of course you're not!' She bent and kissed the top of his head, and she could have sworn that she saw a look of relief on Jed's face.

'Nothing of the sort, Mr. Neil,' he assured the old man 'Melly and I are quite happy to—to wait awhile.'

'Hmm.' The old man regarded him speculatively. 'You're a mighty patient man, it seems to me, Jed Martin. I'd not have been content to keep a lovely girl like Melodie waiting about when I was your age, but I suppose you know your own business best.'

'Grampy——' Melody began, but he was in no mood to be sidetracked.

'I suppose you've not much to worry about out here in the wilds,' he went on. 'There's not so much competition in the way of other young men, is there?'

Jed looked from one to another, as if he suspected some kind of conspiracy, his round face serious as always. 'I'm not worried, Mr. Neil,' he said, but very uncertainly. 'I trust Melly entirely.'

Toothache was something that Melodie had seldom suffered from, so that when she woke up one morning with a dull ache in her jaw she felt worse, perhaps, than many people would have done.

Although it was not really bad, the pain persisted all morning, so that by lunch time she decided to telephone a dentist for an appointment. Fortunately she was able to take up a cancelled appointment and see the dentist that same afternoon.

She left her grandfather in Mrs. Bazeley's able care and went out to catch the bus into Cydale, praying it would mean no more than a filling to placate the trouble. It was a lovely day, and by the time she reached the bus stop her tooth was, needless to say, considerably less painful.

She stood beside the single pole that denoted a fare

132

stage and waited patiently, thinking over what she would have been doing if toothache had not disrupted her routine. So preoccupied was she that she started visibly when a car horn sounded raucously just behind her. She was not altogether surprised to see Keith Scott behind the wheel of the car, and she smiled at the inevitability of it.

'Going my way?' he asked, leaning across to open the passenger door.

Melodie nodded, an action she immediately regretted since it started her tooth throbbing again, and she put a soothing hand to her face. 'I'm going into Cydale, if that's going your way,' she said, and he grinned.

'You name it, I'm going there,' he told her as she climbed in beside him, and he leaned across to close the door after her. 'Something bothering you?' he asked.

She nodded, but less vigorously this time, and wished he was not so close. Really he was the most disconcerting man, especially at close quarters! 'I've got toothache,' she said dolefully.

'Aah! You poor old thing.' He gave her an encouraging smile before letting in the clutch and driving off. 'Is it very bad?'

'Not as bad as it was,' Melodie admitted, 'but I'm hoping he'll just give me a filling. I'm a dreadful coward about going to the dentist and the idea of an extraction petrifies me.'

'And you a nurse?' he teased. 'You should radiate confidence in a situation like this.'

'Not me,' Melodie confessed. 'I just curl up and die.'

'How long will this operation take?' he asked, and she looked at him curiously.

133

'Ooh, I don't know, not very long if it *is* only a filling. Why?'

He turned briefly and grinned. 'You won't feel much like coming home on the bus afterwards,' he said, and she thought she saw his meaning at last.

'I shall feel as right as rain afterwards,' she informed him. 'Unless of course he *does* take the wretched thing out, and I'm hoping he won't.'

'Either way,' he insisted, 'there's no need to hang about waiting for buses when you don't have to. I shan't be very long in Cydale, but if you'll wait I can run you home again.'

Remembering the last time she had been in his company in Cydale she was very dubious about agreeing to the idea although she was tempted, she had to admit. 'I—I don't think I'd better,' she told him at last. 'Thank you just the same.'

He looked at her over one shoulder, obviously suspecting some deep meaning behind her refusal. 'Why not?' he demanded.

'I just don't think I'd better, that's all.'

He grinned at last, and flicked her another glance that mocked her reasons. 'Oh, I see—Jed Martin.'

'In a way,' she admitted. 'Mrs. Martin saw us when —when I had lunch with you.'

'And told him?' She nodded and he clucked his tongue disapprovingly. 'Dear, oh dear, some people do tell tales out of school, don't they?'

'It's not that Jed was unreasonable about it,' she hastened to inform him. 'But he was—well, a bit put out, as you can imagine.'

'I can *well* imagine,' he admitted. 'In his place I'd have been stark staring mad about it.' He grinned at her briefly. 'Only I wouldn't have let it happen in the

134

first place.'

'You couldn't follow me about everywhere I go, any more than Jed can,' she retorted. 'And it was you who said something about him practically keeping me in purdah.'

'So he does, by hiding you away,' he told her. 'It shows a sad lack of self-confidence.'

Melodie frowned at him. 'Must you always be so— so condescending about Jed?' she asked. 'I *am* engaged to him, a fact you seem to forget.'

That quiet laugh tingled her pulse into activity and she looked at him suspiciously. 'I try,' he confessed.

It was almost inevitable that she would agree to ride back with him and his smile recognised as much when he left her at the door of the dentist's surgery, with precise instructions where to find him later. The dentist was confident that only a small filling was required to ease the pain and she faced the coming ordeal with slightly less apprehension.

Glancing at her watch when she left the surgery some time later, she found that she had less time before she was to meet Keith than she had anticipated, and she set off along the short, narrow street towards the car-park at the far end, feeling much better than she had expected. Her toothache was gone and she felt quite lighthearted at having got off so lightly.

She lingered for a few moments by a sweet-shop window and it was while she was studying the temptation of some delicious-looking nut toffee that she saw a passer-by reflected in the plate glass. The woman was coming along the road that turned at an angle to the one she was in and Melodie thought she was as yet unobserved.

There was no mistaking the round, country-red face

135

and white hair of Mrs. Martin and she was coming towards her, might see her at any minute. Without stopping to consider that she was quite alone this time and need have no fear of being seen, Melodie opened the sweet-shop door and went in, glancing hastily back over her shoulder to make sure she had not been seen.

It took only a few minutes to buy some of the toffee that had tempted her from outside and when she came out Mrs. Martin had disappeared, but she was only just in time to arrive first at the car-park. Keith walked up seconds later and smiled knowingly at her.

'I saw you coming out of that tuck-shop,' he told her. 'I hoped you'd had enough sense not to buy any sweets after just coming from the dentist's, but I see I was wrong.'

Melodie gave him a reproachful look, as he unlocked the car and saw her in. 'It was a case of needs must when the devil drives,' she told him. 'I had to duck into the sweet-shop and I could scarcely come out empty-handed.'

'Oh?' He looked interested. 'Don't tell me your Jed is having you followed—how exciting.'

'Oh, don't be such an idiot!' she told him, and laughed despite her reproach. 'I saw Mrs. Martin, Jed's mother, and I didn't want her to see me, especially as I knew it was about time for you to put in an appearance. So I bought some nut toffee.'

'Nut toffee?' He seemed to have forgotten Mrs. Martin. 'Are you crazy? After having toothache?'

'It's my favourite,' Melodie told him, 'and I haven't *got* toothache now.'

He laughed, slamming the car door behind himself, and starting the engine. 'I might have known,' he said resignedly. 'Any other woman would go for pretty boxes of chocolates, but with you it has to be nut toffee.'

She poked her tongue out at him as they turned out of the car-park and immediately realised that she was, as usual, behaving with far more familiarity with him than she should have been. She hoped for a moment that he had not perhaps noticed the gesture while he was busy negotiating his way out of the car-park and into the traffic, but her hope was a vain one, and he turned and grinned at her.

'That,' he informed her, 'was most unladylike, and just what I would expect from a nut toffee type.'

She made no answer, but sat and looked out at the busy streets until they drove through the suburbs and out into the country again. 'You should have turned left there,' she informed him as they turned off the main road and down a small lane with hedges so high on both sides that they kept out the sun and made dappled shadows on their faces as they passed.

'There's a signpost back there,' he said, 'that says Megan's Folly. I see it each time I drive to and from Cydale and it always intrigues me.'

Melodie looked at him curiously, wondering why her heart should suddenly be thudding away against her side, as if she was excited about something. 'So you've decided to go and see it today,' she guessed, and he nodded.

'I have a local expert with me,' he told her, 'and I'd like to go and see what a folly looks like. I've never seen one, and the idea of them seems so utterly British that I feel I really ought to see one.'

'I don't think it's a condition of naturalisation, is it?' she asked, and laughed when he pulled a face.

'I sincerely hope not,' he told her, 'otherwise I shall

fall far short. I thought you might fill that particular gap in my education,' he added hopefully. 'I presume you know Megan's Folly?'

'Yes, I know it,' she admitted. 'But I'm not at all sure that I should be on my way there now. I'm expected back for tea.'

'Well, how long does it take to look at a folly?'

She smiled. 'No time at all,' she said. 'It's only a ruined wall with wild flowers growing on top.' It was also a reminder of her childhood, but she did not tell him that yet.

'Then you've got plenty of time,' he informed her, 'because you won't be expected back until bus time.'

'Oh, I see, you've got it all worked out, have you?'

The blue eyes glinted at her wickedly over his shoulder as he smiled. 'Of course,' he said. 'My education's been neglected far too long, folly-wise, and it isn't often I have the opportunity to consult an expert, so I'm making the most of it.' He negotiated another sharp corner in the narrow lane. 'You don't mind, do you?'

'Not really,' she said. 'But if you don't slow down you'll drive straight past without seeing it. There— that next gate.'

She pointed to a five-barred gate, giving access to a meadow, and he turned the car on to the grass verge and cut the engine. The silence fell over them like a veil and they sat for a moment without saying a word to break it.

'Are you coming?' he asked then, and she nodded.

She felt sure she was being extremely rash in coming here with him and Jed would be most disapproving if he knew, but nevertheless she found herself following his tall, rangy figure through the gate and into the field beyond.

The ground rose after a few feet and the folly, as much as was left of it, stood on the brow of the rise overlooking lush green pasture and the moors beyond. From the top of the ruined wall, now no more than a few feet high, the view was breathtaking and when she had come there with her grandfather as a child she remembered him lifting her high on to the wall so that she could not only see better but also pick some of the flowers from the top. He had been a big, healthily strong man then, and easily able to lift her and climb up beside her.

The ruined walls of grey stone had a sad, neglected look which the bright scarlet poppies growing on the top and in the crevices did their best to relieve. Melodie led the way inside the four crumbling walls and looked around her with a faint smile of remembering.

'I thought you'd know your way around it,' Keith told her. 'Do you know who Megan was too?'

She nodded. 'Yes, as it happens, I do.'

'Tell me?' The tone was persuasive and she hesitated only briefly.

'All part of your education?' she asked, and smiled. He nodded. 'Well, to begin with, Megan was a Welsh girl, as you might guess from her name, but her father farmed most of the land round here, he was a wealthy man and doted on her. She fell in love with a young blacksmith who came from the village on the other side of the moor from here.'

'Ah, a love story.' The blue eyes glowed darkly in the shadowy ghost of the folly.

Melodie looked at him, her hands feeling oddly trembly as she clasped them together in front of her. 'Don't you want to hear it if it's a love story?' she asked.

'Certainly I do, I'm a very romantic turn of mind, you know.'

'Are you? I didn't——' She hastily lowered her eyes and went on with her story. 'It seems this young man used to visit her every night, no matter what the weather, and she used to wait for him here, on the brow of this hill, until one night in winter he disappeared. There was deep snow on the moor, but he set off as usual to see Megan and he was never seen again. Megan never recovered from the shock and she had this tower built so that she could look for him coming across the moor. She finally died here, many years later, still waiting for him to come.'

'Aah!' He made a sad face, teasing her for her seriousness. 'Do you believe in such romantic follies, Melodie?'

'I don't know.' She shrugged uneasily. 'It's supto be true, and I suppose there are people who—who love someone as wholeheartedly as that.'

'Very likely,' he agreed surprisingly, and cocked a curious brow at her. 'Who told you about it?'

She looked at him questioningly. 'My grandfather, why?'

He smiled. 'I just wondered.'

'He used to bring me here when I was a little girl,' she told him, 'and I used to get poppies from the top of the wall and take them home to my grannie.'

He glanced up at the delicate red poppies fluttering in the warm breeze, and smiled. 'Do you want to take some home now?' he asked, and she looked at him uncertainly.

'I—I can't reach them.'

'You couldn't when you were a little girl,' he told

140

her, 'but you got them then, didn't you? How did you reach them before?'

'Grampy lifted me up to pick them.'

He held out his hands, a glint of challenge in his blue eyes. 'I'll lift you.'

'No—no, I couldn't, I'm not a little girl now.'

'I'm not your grandfather either,' he said softly, 'but I can lift a little creature like you with no trouble at all. Come on, Melodie, what are you afraid of?' He laughed when she merely looked at him in silence, horribly uncertain and wishing her pulse would not race so wildly. It was madness to have come here with him and she wanted to get away as fast as she could, only something held her there still. He looked down at her half mocking, half encouraging. 'I'll go up first, how's that?'

He climbed up on to the broken wall and reached down his hands for her. 'Keith——'

'Ups-a-daisy!' She was hauled bodily up on to the wall and, for a moment of panic at the height, clung on to him, gaining confidence when the enchantment of the view distracted her.

It was breathtaking and seemed to go on for ever. The streams weaving in and out of the valleys and hills, slithering across the moors and catching the sun as they twisted and turned. The wider shimmer of a river somewhere too distant to guess, hazy in the autumn sun, and a sky as blue as any that early summer had to offer but less clear with the misty promise of autumn. It hadn't changed at all and she looked at it in silence, too moved for words, only just aware of the arm encircling her waist as if to steady her.

'O.K.?'

She turned, startled for the moment, and found the

blue eyes disturbingly close. 'Yes, yes, thank you.' There was a strange kind of excitement in her and one which she dared not analyse too closely as, laughing a little harshly, she moved out of his hold.

'There's a funny sort of feeling about this place, isn't there?' she asked.

He smiled but not in mockery, more a kind of understanding. 'Maybe it's the ghost of poor old Megan,' he suggested. 'Perhaps she's still here waiting for her lover.'

Melodie shivered involuntarily. 'Maybe it's our imagination,' she said. 'I never noticed it when I was little.'

'Perhaps you were less in rapport with the feelings of lovers,' he suggested quietly, and she hastily turned away rather than meet his eyes.

'Nothing's really changed,' she said. 'Although there seem to be a lot more poppies than there used to be.'

She heard him laugh softly. 'It's the law of nature,' he told her. 'Everything multiplies.'

She plucked the scarlet poppies with unsteady fingers, knowing they would wilt before she got them home as they had always done, but delighting in the soft prettiness of them held close together in her hand. She heard a faint movement somewhere behind her and thought he must have moved further round the wall. It was quite a surprise to see him down below her, standing inside the folly again, and she stood up, looking at him uncertainly.

The blue of the sky behind her, silhouetted her like a small, colourful statue, the bright red poppies and her mass of copper-red hair looking very similar to sun-hazed eyes. She stood looking down at him for a second, her heart fluttering wildly with what she thought was fear of being alone up there, then she reached out her arms to him, almost unthinkingly.

'Help me down,' she said.

He looked up at her, the blue eyes shadowed in the dim interior of the folly, making no move to help her down, then he smiled slowly. 'Suppose I don't?' he asked, and she shook her head.

'Then I'd jump down and probably break a leg.'

'Would you really be so rash?'

'Rash or not,' Melodie told him, 'I've no intention of staying here all day.'

'You're not prepared to waste away like poor Megan?'

'Definitely not!'

'Hmm.' He was still smiling, but still not offering his help. 'If you did,' he informed her, 'they might rename it Melodie's Folly.' He was laughing now, standing with his feet apart, hands on his hips and an expression in his eyes that she could not quite determine.

'Keith——'

He stood for a moment longer watching her, as if the sight of her against the pale sky was something he wanted to remember, then he reached up his hands for her and lifted her down, setting her gently on her feet and keeping hold on her. 'You see,' he told her softly. 'I can lift you easily.'

Melodie put her hands over his trying to free herself. 'I never doubted it,' she told him, 'now will you please let go of me?'

'If I must.' She looked down at her bouquet of poppies, seeking a distraction from the disturbing gaze he fixed her with, gently touching the paper-thin petals with one finger.

'They always droop,' she said sadly, 'it's such a

143

shame.'

'Then why do you pick them?'

She glanced up, her eyes curious and a small frown between her brows. 'I don't really know,' she confessed. 'It's just that they're so beautiful I feel—I feel as if they'll never die.'

He put a hand gently against her cheek and smiled.

'You're a funny little thing,' he said softly, 'and I'd better get you home before——' His laugh trickled along her spine again and he shook his head slowly. 'Come on, copper-nob, we've had enough folly for one day.'

CHAPTER EIGHT

IT was almost impossible not to tell her grandfather about their visit to Megan's Folly, but Melodie made as little of it as possible. Nevertheless the old man looked at her shrewdly and seemed quite amused at the idea of her having been with Keith Scott again.

'Better not let your Jed know about *that* little escapade,' he told her with much raising of eyebrows and a wicked glint in his eyes. 'That wouldn't go down at all well, I reckon.'

'It wasn't an escapade, as you call it,' Melodie objected.

'I never was much of a man for my books,' the old man retorted slyly, 'but it seems to me I remember old Bill Shakespeare saying something about somebody protesting too much.'

'I don't know why I bother to tell you anything,'

Melodie told him. 'You always put your own interpretation on it, and it's usually the wrong one.'

'Like your Jed,' he said, and chuckled dryly at her flush of embarrassment.

'There's absolutely no need why Jed should know I've been to the folly at all unless you tell him,' she said. 'It was all so straightforward, but some people seem intent on making a mountain out of a molehill. Keith wanted to see what a folly looked like and we went and looked at it, that's all. It's hardly what you call an escapade.'

'You brought me some poppies like you used to for your grannie,' he said. 'That was sweet of you, lass.' He looked at the rather sad-looking flowers, out of their element now without their natural, precarious background and the sun and wind to give them life.

Melodie lifted a drooping red bloom with one finger. 'I shouldn't have brought them really,' she said. 'They never last very long once they're picked.'

'Nostalgia's a good reason,' the old man told her gently, and looked at her in what she called his sly way. 'Did you pick them yourself?'

'Yes, of course I——' She bit her lip when she realised where she had been led.

'Of course you're bigger now than when I took you,' he went on, blandly innocent, 'but I wouldn't have thought you could reach them on the top of that wall, lass.'

'You know quite well I couldn't, Grampy.'

'Mmm.' He looked thoughtful. 'I suppose he could lift you easily enough, a big feller like that.'

'He climbed up first and hauled me up after him,' Melodie told him shortly. 'My ascent wasn't very elegant, I might add.'

145

'Nonsense,' her grandfather told her. 'You couldn't be inelegant if you tried.'

'Well, it's nothing to make a big issue about,' she said, 'and I'd—I'd just as soon Jed didn't know, Grampy.'

She looked at him, half defiant, half appealing, and a dry laugh crackled in his throat. 'This is where I came in,' he reminded her, 'only you've been busy ever since trying to convince me that it didn't matter.'

'It's not important,' Melodie insisted, 'it's just that —well, Jed might not understand.'

'And his mother would understand even less,' her grandfather added, and reached for her hand so that she came and stood beside his chair, realising that the old man understood her probably better than anyone alive. 'Melodie, you're not taking on more than you can manage there, are you?'

'More than—oh no, of course not, Grampy.' She held on to his hand, but did not look at him for fear he should read something into her words that wasn't meant to be there. 'Mrs. Martin's been looking after Jed and Michael ever since Jed's wife died, I suppose she makes—well, a bit more fuss of them than she should, but I—I shan't try and take over Michael's upbringing, it wouldn't be fair after all this time.'

'She's not likely to take kindly to another woman coming into her household,' the old man said quietly, watching her face. 'It could be very uncomfortable for you, lass.'

She shook her head, reluctant to face the prospect now as she always was. 'I'll be very careful, Grampy, I know how she'll feel after all this time.'

The shrewd but tired old eyes watched her for a

moment in silence, then he shook his head slowly. 'I just hope he proves worth it, lass, that's all.'

It was sheer bad luck that Melodie should run foul of Maria Santas on that particular afternoon when she was on her way to see Jed. Unfortunate, especially, that the other girl should make her protest just at the moment Jed arrived.

Melodie had not even realised she was coming up behind her, but as she reached the outer limits of the spinney the black, Diablo, came racing up at full gallop and was reined in sharply only just before he ran her down.

Melodie turned startled eyes and saw her antagonist high above her, looking at her down her arrogant nose as always. 'You—Melodie Neil!' Maria got her tongue round the name with some difficulty and the black eyes glittered like a jet in the hard, beautiful face.

'Miss Santas?' She tried to sound calm and unprovoked, but it was difficult.

'I see you.' The meaning, apart from the obvious one, escaped Melodie for the moment and she merely looked at her queryingly, hearing Jed's approach through the spinney.

'I—I don't quite understand,' she said, turning with relief to smile at Jed. 'Do you know Mr. Martin?' she asked. 'Jed, this is Miss Santas, Mr. Scott's—visitor.' She had almost said fiancée, but the absence of an engagement ring was, she noticed now, a fact.

Jed would have shaken hands, but the chilling nod he received by way of recognition discouraged him and he too looked at the girl curiously. 'You too have make me go from your land,' she told him. 'I have no wish

147

to meet you.'

'You're on *my* land now,' Melodie reminded her shortly.

Maria Santas looked down her haughty nose at her. 'I see you yesterday,' she said. She struggled with both her English and her temper, but Melodie at last saw the light and and glanced hastily at Jed.

'You probably did see me, Miss Santas,' she admitted, deciding to brazen it out now that it was started. 'I wasn't trying to hide.'

'Hide? What is this hide?'

Melodie felt something akin to panic with Maria's ruthless black eyes on her from one direction and Jed's curious ones from another. 'I mean,' she tried to explain, 'that I—I didn't mind being seen.'

'So!' Maria too saw the light. 'You do not care, huh? You ride with Carlos and you do not care who—who see you? You are shameless, no?'

'No, I'm not!' Melodie denied staunchly, seeing Jed's interest growing. She had told him that Maria called Keith by his second name of Carlos, so he would have no difficulty in putting two and two together. 'I've done nothing to be ashamed of, Miss Santas.'

'No?' The black eyes glowed angrily. 'You are to *marry* this—this *hombre*, no? And already you make a fool of him.' The black gaze turned on Jed, and her thin lips curled disdainfully. '*Loco!*' she said with such obvious meaning that Jed's face flushed with anger.

'Now look here, young woman——' he began, but Maria was in no mood to listen, and her attention was already back with Melodie. 'You stay away from Carlos,' she ordered imperiously, 'or you will be very,

very sorry—you will see.'

'I did not——'

'*Esté quieta!*' The sharp voice silenced her momentarily, but Melodie's anger was almost as furious as her antagonist's now and her green eyes shone with it as she sought for words.

'Don't you dare speak to me like that,' she said. 'And get off our land, you have no right here. Go back where you belong, Miss Santas.'

'*Perra! Rústica!*' The riding crop she carried in one hand was aimed at Melodie's face, but a hastily raised arm took the two sharp blows instead and when it was lowered she saw Maria already riding like fury across the meadow, the black going at full gallop.

Melodie nursed her arm, biting her lip on the sharp sting of two bright red weals already showing on her light skin, but Jed seemed far more concerned with other matters and he watched Maria's departure with his eyes narrowed and his brows drawn together.

'What was all that about, Melly?' he asked at last.

'I would have thought it was obvious,' Melodie said, annoyed that he should be showing so little concern for her having borne the brunt of Maria's temper.

He looked at her still frowning. 'I gather from what that woman said that she's seen you with Scott again, yesterday.' His eyes narrowed when she did not answer him. 'Is that what she was so angry about, Melly?'

'Yes, of course it was, you heard what she said.'

'Were you with him yesterday?'

She flushed, biting her lip and feeling very close to tears, though whether from self-pity or sheer temper she could not quite decide. Either way she did not relish being cross-examined by Jed, having just been

149

put through fire by Maria Santas. 'I was with Keith for a while yesterday,' she told him, 'but there's a perfectly simple explanation for it. He——'

'There always is,' Jed said sharply without giving her time to finish what she was going to say. 'You know quite well how I feel about you being with Scott and yet you were with him again yesterday. Why, for heaven's sake?'

'Because I had little option,' Melodie retorted, curling her fingers round the marks on her arm, feeling as if she must either burst into tears soon or else hit out at someone. 'I had toothache and he ran me into Cydale to the dentist, that's all.'

'*He* did?' He looked completely bewildered. 'Why on earth did you ask him? Why not me?'

'Oh, you idiot!' she cried. 'I didn't ask him to. I was at the bus stop and he came along and gave me a lift. He also brought me back because his affairs in Cydale and my time at the dentist took about the same time, and that's all there is to it. Now for heaven's sake, Jed, let it drop, I'm sick of the subject!' She thought ruefully of how she had been so careful to avoid letting his mother see her and now Maria had let the cat out of the bag and achieved the same object.

'Well, I think it's time I had something to say to *Mr*. Scott,' he declared stubbornly. 'I'm not very convinced by coincidences, Melly, even if you are, and —Melly!'

He called the last after her in a kind of desperation, but Melodie was running across the meadow towards the house, the tears at last running down her face. She would no longer stay and listen to stupid accusations which had no basis in fact, and she did not care what Maria Santas or Jed thought about it.

She ran most of the way back to the house and arrived dishevelled and breathless so that Mrs. Bazeley looked up in surprise when she came into the kitchen. 'Is owt wrong, Miss Neil?' she asked, but Melodie shook her head, too short of breath to speak yet. She paused by the kitchen table to put her hands to her hair and try to bring some semblance of order to it before she went to see her grandfather. If anyone would see her side of it, Grampy would, and she would tell him all about her encounter with Maria.

'I haven't got tea yet,' the housekeeper told her. 'It's a bit early yet.'

'Oh yes, of course, Mrs. Bazeley, it's quite all right.' She was aware of the woman's eyes on her flushed cheeks and tear-wet eyes and hastily brushed a hand across her eyes.

'Are you all right, lass?' She was kind and homely for all her usually blunt manner, and Melodie smiled reassuringly, nodding her head.

'I'm O.K., Mrs. Bazeley, don't worry,' she told her, 'and there's no rush for tea, it isn't time yet.'

It was only when she reached the sitting-room door that she realised that the tea-tray on the table just near the kitchen door had been laid for three, and she was uncertain as she opened the door whether it was pleasure or dismay that made her heart skip rapidly when Keith Scott got to his feet.

Her grandfather's keen eyes soon spotted her tearful dishevelment, but not as soon as his visitor did. The blue eyes narrowed fractionally and he looked at her as if he too would start questioning her. 'Melodie——' He saw the marks on her arm then and lifted the arm in a grip that defied her efforts to evade

151

it. 'What happened?' he demanded.

Her grandfather, it seemed, was content to leave all the questioning to Keith, but Melodie was not having any more, even if their intentions were for the best. 'Now don't *you* start—grilling me,' she told him, trying to free her arm from that iron grip. 'I've had enough for one day!'

'It's obvious what made those marks,' he told her quietly, 'and I wasn't thinking of grilling you, as you call it. For one thing, I haven't the right—that's Jed Martin's privilege, but if he's been abusing his privilege like this I'll certainly have——' He shook his head, the black frown easing gradually. 'I still don't have the right,' he told her quietly.

Her grandfather looked at her steadily for a moment. '*Did* he do that, lass?' he asked.

'Oh no, of course not!' She looked quite appalled at the idea, so much so that they were bound to believe her.

'It's just as well,' Keith observed, and released his hold on her arm while Melodie wondered what he would have done if it *had* been Jed and not Maria. He looked back at the old man and shook his head slowly. 'I don't think Martin would actually hurt her,' he told him. 'It must have been Maria.' The blue eyes flicked quickly and compellingly back to Melodie. 'It was, wasn't it, Melodie?'

She nodded. 'She—she saw us coming back yesterday and she was furious.'

'I know.' The small tight smile round his mouth was quite unlike his usual beam. 'I had my share yesterday.'

Melodie looked startled for a moment. 'She—she didn't hit *you*, did she?'

He laughed shortly at the idea of that, as she might

have known he would. 'She wouldn't dare,' he told her, and she knew he meant it. 'So she took it out on you, did she?'

'I certainly came in for the brunt of it.'

'I'm sorry.'

'I don't see why,' Melodie told him. 'It was as much my fault as yours that we were together for allowing myself to be persuaded. I shouldn't have come with you.'

His grin was almost back to normal and the blue eyes teased her. 'You hadn't much choice, had you?' he asked.

'That's what I tried to tell Jed, only——'

'He didn't believe you?' he guessed, when she stopped in mid-sentence. 'Well, I'm not sure I can blame him.'

'I—I think he believes me in a way,' she told him, 'but—well, mostly he blames you for——.' Again she was forced to break off, unable to find the right words, and he laughed softly.

'I don't blame *him*,' he told her. 'In his place I'd be ready to do battle for you, but your Jed isn't the battling sort, is he?'

'Definitely not!' her grandfather averred, and Melodie flushed, cross because Jed was rapidly becoming the villain of the piece and that was not what she wanted no matter what he had done to annoy her just now.

'Jed's too kind and gentle to go around fighting anyone,' she said firmly. 'And that's the way I like him.'

'Nobody's arguing the point, girl,' her grandfather told her. 'You know your own mind best, I expect, although it's not a female trait, as I'm sure Keith will agree.'

Melodie flushed, her chin high. 'I don't doubt Keith will agree,' she said. She had noticed the use of the visitor's first name and thought how much more friendly her grandfather was with Keith than he was with Jed.

Keith smiled slowly. 'I'd better keep silent on that point, I think, Mr. Neil,' he remarked. 'There seems to be another storm brewing.' He pulled a face at the old man and the two of them burst into laughter, leaving Melodie feeling angry and odd man out, with her fists curled at her sides.

'Very funny,' she declared shortly. 'I'm glad you two find it so amusing.'

'Oh, come on, lass,' the old man chided her. 'You can take a joke as well as the next man—or you used to.'

'I—I still can.' She felt tearful again suddenly and her arm ached abominably so that she instinctively covered it with her hand, looking at them with reproachful eyes.

Keith noted the gesture and frowned again. 'Is it very painful, Melodie?' he asked, and she nodded.

'Your Miss Santas wasn't pulling her punches,' she told him. 'I'm only glad I managed to get my arm up and protect my face.'

'Your face?' The blue eyes glowed with an anger more virulent than anything she had seen before and she felt a momentary chill of fear at the sight of it. 'Do you mean she actually aimed at your face?'

Melodie nodded slowly, uncertain in the circumstances whether she should tell him so much. 'She—she was very angry and I don't think——'

'I know Maria,' he interrupted brusquely. 'I'll see her when I get back and leave her in no doubt how I

154

feel about her behaviour.'

'You——' She could not put her fears into words, but she was still overawed and a little afraid of the anger she had seen in his eyes.

'I'll speak to her,' he said. 'It's time——' He shrugged and a tight smile touched his wide mouth. 'It's time the air was cleared.'

'Please don't make any trouble on my account,' Melodie pleaded, but he looked adamant.

'No more than is long overdue,' he said, and Melodie shook her head.

'I—I suppose, in a way, I don't really blame her for being so angry,' she said. 'I would have told her that—that she had no cause to worry, not in that direction, but I had no opportunity.'

'I can imagine,' he said wryly.

'Was Jed Martin there when this happened?' her grandfather asked.

'Yes.'

'And what did he do about it?'

She knew he was waiting for her to admit that Jed had done nothing about it, not even about Maria's vicious attack, although he had had little enough time after that, heaven knows, but she didn't let them know that he had not said a word of consolation for her painful arm. 'There wasn't much he could do, Grampy. There wasn't much anyone could do, it was all over so quickly. Anyway,' she added, trying to sound more cheerful, 'I'm not very much worse for the encounter, although my arm's painful.'

'Well, you look as if you've been pulled through a hedge, my lass,' the old man informed her bluntly. 'And you're back very early too, aren't you? Have you had a fight with your feller as well?'

Melodie was very conscious of Keith Scott's interest in the subject as well and she stuck out her chin stubbornly. She had no intention of letting him be a party to any more of her private affairs. Her eyes were reproachful when she looked at her grandfather.

'I don't think my—my business can possibly be of much interest to Mr.—to Keith,' she told him. 'And I'd much prefer not to discuss my affairs and Jed's with anyone, Grampy.'

'Please yourself, my girl,' the old man retorted. 'But go and get yourself tidied up before teatime or you'll spoil all our appetites.'

'Is—is Keith staying for tea?' she asked, knowing the answer full well.

'Of course he's staying for tea,' the old man told her.

'I just wondered,' Melodie said blithely. 'It's a bit of a puzzle to me how he manages to run a farm with all the time he spends here with you.'

'You——' The old man looked as if he was about to explode and she realised that she had been very rash in making him so angry. As his nurse she should have known better. 'You mind your manners, my girl,' he managed at last. 'Keith knows what he's doing and he's as good a farmer as anyone in this neck of the woods I'll take wager.'

'I get by,' Keith agreed quietly, but his eyes were bright with the customary laughter when he looked at her. 'Does it bother you having me come to see your grandfather, Melodie?'

'Bother me?' She stared at him for a moment and read all manner of things into the expression in his eyes before she hastily lowered her own. 'Of course it doesn't,' she told him. 'Come as often as you like as long as it doesn't overtire Grampy.'

'I try not to,' he assured her solemnly. 'But he's a mine of information and we swop notes.'

'It's like old times in the market pub,' her grandfather vowed. 'He knows his sheep, this feller.'

'I thought cattle were your—your family's business,' she said, looking at him curiously.

'So they are, but I spent quite a lot of time in a very sparsely populated area of South America called Patagonia where they have huge sheep farms, as well as working over here for various farmers before I set up on my own.' The blue eyes smiled at her. 'I learned the hard way, Melodie.'

'I—I didn't say you didn't,' she told him, feeling as if she had been thoroughly chastened.

'Oh, all right, I forgive you, in that case.'

She stared at him, taunted by that elusive laughter, then she went out of the room without another word, closing the door noisily behind her and wondering why it was she felt a strange sense of exhilaration as she went upstairs to her room.

Melodie was not too surprised when she answered a knock on the front door next morning to find Jed on the step, his expression a strange mixture of apology and stubbornness, and she stood back to let him in.

'Melly.' He looked at her for a moment, obviously uncertain what to say or do, then he took her hands and drew her towards him, his eyes searching her face for some hint of how she felt, but she kept her own gaze lowered. 'I'm sorry.' He bent his head and kissed her gently on her forehead.

'You don't have to be sorry, Jed.' She looked up at him. 'I was the one who was in the wrong, wasn't I?'

157

'No, not wrong,' he denied. 'You couldn't help being persuaded by Scott, I can see that now, I shouldn't have blamed you.'

'Not even for allowing myself to be persuaded?' she asked. 'That's as bad, isn't it?'

Jed shook his head. 'No, not really,' he said. 'That's why I'm not really blaming you. I told you Scott was a man who'd get his own way with women. I recognise that type, they're so blatantly obvious.'

'Not to me, evidently,' she told him, and felt his fingers tighten their hold on her arms.

'I see.'

'Jed——' She sought for words, but found none that would make any sense to him. No amount of explaining to him that Keith came to Millway to see her grandfather would convince him. 'I—I suppose you're right in one way,' she admitted. 'I should have had more sense than to go with him, but I had such wretched toothache and I never like that bus ride into Cydale at the best of times. The offer of a lift *was* tempting, and I'm afraid I took the easy way out.'

'Of course.' He kissed her again, this time on her mouth, and Melodie wondered briefly if competition had finally stirred Jed from his matter-of-fact acceptance of her. 'You won't see him again,' he added, and she frowned.

'I don't quite see how I can promise that, Jed, when he comes here to see Grampy. They're very friendly and Grampy would miss his visits now.'

He frowned. 'Does he often come here to the house?'

'Fairly often,' she said, remembering her jibe yesterday after his spending so much time at Millway. 'They talk sheep, apparently, and it makes Grampy feel like old times, I just haven't the heart to try and stop the visits when he enjoys them so much.'

The hazel eyes looked at her with a speculative gleam in them. 'As long as you're sure it's for your grandfather's sake that you don't object to him coming.'

'Of course it is.' She sounded genuinely indignant that he should suggest anything else, but she *had* rather changed her mind about her grandfather having visitors, although she convinced herself that it was because Keith was quiet and did not get the old man too excited or stay long enough to tire him.

'I don't like the idea of him coming too often,' he said, running the matter into the ground as always.

'He can't come too often,' Melodie told him, an edge of impatience already on her voice. 'He has Maria Santas and her mother there.'

'That woman!' He looked down at her arm and saw the red weals of yesterday turned to reddish blue bruises. 'Did she hurt you, Melly?'

The concern was rather belated, but she could not find it in her heart to blame him too much. Women like Maria Santas were far outside Jed's experience and he would quite probably not have realised how much strength and spite she had put into the attack.

She smiled ruefully. 'It does hurt when somebody puts their mind to it as Maria did,' she told him. 'Although it's not quite so bad now.'

'Crowd of damned foreigners,' Jed declared, with uncharacteristic vehemence. 'Why don't they clear off back to where they belong?'

She could not resist a smile at that, for it was obvious he included Keith in the 'damned foreigners'. She could, she supposed, have told him about Keith's plans

159

to become naturalised, but this was not the moment and instead she smiled and shook her head.

'That doesn't sound much like the Yorkshire hospitality we're always boasting about,' she told him. 'And,' she looked at him from under her lashes, 'I don't think you'd have so much objection to Maria if it wasn't for Keith, would you?'

He frowned. 'Keith?' He repeated the name as if he disliked it as much as he did its bearer. 'You seem to be on more—friendly terms with him than anyone else in the village, Melly. I've never heard anyone else refer to him by his christian name.'

She looked at him uneasily for a moment. 'Grampy does,' she said, and he frowned again.

'Your grandfather,' he stated firmly, 'has a lot less discrimination than I gave him credit for. I'd have thought he'd have spotted Scott for what he was and disliked him on sight.'

'Oh, no, Jed!' She shook her head, quite sure of her facts. 'How could he dislike him, he's so very much like him, or like Grampy was as a younger man. They're so much alike he couldn't possibly dislike him.'

She did not even notice the look on Jed's face when she said it, she was so involved in recognising the same characteristics in the two men under discussion. She had never before realised how alike they were and she was not at all sure that the realisation was a comfort to her.

CHAPTER NINE

'OH, it's you.' Melodie held the door open wide to admit Keith Scott, but he pulled a rueful face over his welcome.

'I gather I'm not the most welcome visitor, am I right?'

'At the moment,' Melodie confessed, 'no one's very welcome. Mrs. Bazeley's sister has been rushed into hospital and she's gone charging off to play foster-mum to about six children and a husband, so I'm head cook-housekeeper as well as nurse.'

'Oh, I'm sorry. Is there anything I can do to help?'

She looked at the light trousers and white shirt he wore and smiled wryly. 'I doubt if you're dressed for potato-peeling,' she told him, 'and you'd probably waste half of them anyway. No, thanks, I can manage.'

'Independent as ever,' he grinned, and she lifted her chin.

'I have to be. Now if you'll excuse my lack of host-essly charm, I'll leave you to find your own way in to Grampy and get on with this pie.' She waved floury hands at him. 'Some people choose the most awkward times to call.'

'What sort of pie?' he asked, as she turned away, and she looked at him suspiciously.

'Steak and kidney—why?'

'With that thick, crumbly sort of pastry on top?'

She nodded, turning to face him again, her floury hands on her hips and a streak of flour down one cheek.

'Flaky pastry,' she agreed. 'And I still say—why?'

The blue eyes looked unbelievably appealing and he had an expression that could have been called soulful except that his were not the type of features that could have been described by anything so pious. 'If your pastry's as good as your cakes,' he told her, 'you've got a hungry man on your hands.'

'But you *can't* stay,' Melodie objected, almost succumbing to the laughter that welled up inside her. 'You've got guests, you can't just stay out for dinner like that.'

'Not any longer I haven't,' he told her quietly, obviously waiting for her reaction.

'Oh?' She was wary now, and uncertain whether or not she was pleased about it.

He nodded, his dark face shadowed in the dimness of the hall. 'Maria and her mother left this morning. I took them to the airport and saw them off.'

She stood for a moment in silence, wondering how willingly Maria Santas had gone, and if she would be coming back again some day to marry Keith. There were a thousand and one questions she wanted to ask, but it was not possible to ask them, not now. 'I'm sorry,' was all she could find to say, and he arched a curious brow over that.

'Sorry?' he asked.

'You'll—you'll miss her, won't you?'

'Yes,' he admitted thoughtfully, 'I will. I've known Maria a long time.'

He did not volunteer any further information and she felt reticent about saying too much, remembering how he had vowed only the other days to settle things once and for all with Maria. That was immediately after she had fallen foul of the other girl and wondered

162

if that incident had in any way precipitated Maria's departure, unable to help feeling a little guilty about it.

'I'm sorry.'

'So you said.' He was still far less concerned about it than he should have been, she felt, and frowned.

'I mean it, Keith. I'd hate to think that—well, you did say something about speaking to her the other day about—about what happened.'

'When she hit you.'

'I'd hate to think you quarrelled over that and that's why she's gone back to South America.'

'It contributed,' he admitted. 'But it also cleared the air on a good many other things as well, so you needn't get feeling guilty about it.'

'But——'

'One person at least well be delighted to see Maria back in San Felipe,' he said, and Melodie looked at him curiously. He smiled knowingly. 'My brother Juan; he's been crazy about Maria ever since they were at school, and I'm sure he'll be only too happy to console her injured pride.'

She looked at him and frowned. 'Are you sure that's all it will be, Keith? Injured pride?'

He nodded quite firmly. 'Quite sure,' he averred in that voice that defied argument. 'She'll be just as happy with my brother.'

'I—I didn't know you had a brother.'

He grinned. 'I've got four, actually. There's never any shortage of sons in our family.'

'No girls?'

He shook his head, his eyes glistening. 'I'm planning to change all that when I start a family,' he informed her confidently. 'There hasn't been a daughter born

163

in the Scott family for nearly a hundred years.'

'When you start a family?' she echoed. 'And you've sent Maria back to South America?'

The blue eyes looked at her steadily so that she hastily lowered her own. 'There are other women in the world besides Maria,' he said softly.

She felt her fingers curl into her palms and hastily sought to change the subject. 'Won't your mother miss you when you become—British?' she asked, and he shook his head.

'My mother died when Nico, my youngest brother, was born,' he told her. 'It's my grandmother who makes the decisions and she decided to send me to England to be schooled, a bit, I suspect, because she's about a quarter English, and she heartily approves of my becoming the complete Englishman. It's only Father who doesn't agree.'

'Because you're the eldest son and have the family name?'

He smiled. 'Smart girl! Yes, he wouldn't have minded so much if it had been Arturo or Juan, but I take the family name with me, and he and Maria's father had set their hearts on our marrying from the time we were children.'

'Oh, I see.'

'Don't worry about Maria,' he told her confidently. 'She'll settle quite happily for Juan, once she gets used to the idea.'

'I don't know how you can be so sure of that,' she told him a little reproachfully. 'You sound completely ruthless about swopping the poor girl around.'

'Not as ruthless as I'd have been keeping her here on a Yorkshire farm,' he told her. 'Maria needs her own environment. I could no more expect her to be happy here than I could—could take you to the dust and heat of San Felipe.'

She looked startled for a second. 'No—no, of course not.'

He laughed softly, setting her pulse hammering wildly at her temple. 'Anyway, it would never work with Maria over here. I tried to put them off coming, but'—he shrugged—'the idea was for her to persuade me not to go on with the naturalisation idea and to go back with her to San Felipe. The trouble is I'm so thoroughly English now and she doesn't understand the English at all.'

'Does she think we're all peasants?' she asked. 'That is more or less what *rústica* means, isn't it?'

He nodded. 'Is that what she called you?'

'On more than one occasion,' she agreed. 'I suspect she called me something considerably worse than that on the day Michael and I had our picnic by the lake, didn't she?'

'Much worse,' he agreed without hesitation, and she remembered his angry berating of the girl and her hasty withdrawal.

Neither of them spoke for a minute until Melodie could no longer stand the meaningful silence and turned away again. 'I must finish that wretched pie,' she said, 'or we'll never get dinner tonight.'

'We?'

She paused with her hand on the kitchen door handle, turning to look at him over one shoulder a gleam of laughter in her eyes. 'Me and Grampy,' she told him.

'Oh.'

She laughed then and saw the responsive gleam in his eyes when he smiled. 'And you too if you want to stay,' she told him. 'I might just as well invite you because you'll only work your way round Grampy if I don't.'

'Quite likely,' he agreed, and was beside her in a couple of strides. He bent his head and kissed her gently beside her mouth, his eyes darkly blue in the dim light. 'Thank you, *amada*.'

It was quite late for her grandfather to be up when Keith left Millway and Melodie saw him to the door with mixed feelings. His company did wonders for her grandfather's spirits, but if he was likely to come over more often now that Maria and her mother had gone, it would make things very difficult for her with Jed.

She tried to tell herself that there was no foundation for Jed's suspicions of him, but it was becoming more and more difficult to convince herself and twice as difficult to convince Jed. He learned of the departure of Maria and her mother with his usual expression and frowned as if it puzzled him.

'They've not been here long, have they?' he said.

'About a month,' Melodie informed him. 'Quite a long time really.'

Jed shook his head, unconvinced. 'Not so long when you think of the distance and the expense of coming over here. I wonder why they've suddenly decided to leave. Did he say?'

'Not really,' Melodie said, unwilling even to think that she had, at least in part, been responsible for Maria Santas going home.

'Well, it's a pity he didn't go with them,' Jed declared bluntly.

'Oh, he won't be going back,' she told him. 'Not permanently anyway.'

166

'Oh?' he eyed her curiously. 'You seem very well informed.'

'I—I don't suppose it's exactly a secret,' she said. 'After all, it has to appear in a public notice or something, doesn't it? Asking anyone if they have grounds for objection. I've seen them in the papers quite often.'

'What *are* you talking about?' Jed asked. 'What on earth have public notices to do with Scott not going back to—to wherever he came from?'

'He's applied for naturalisation,' Melodie told him.

'Good grief!' he exclaimed, staring at her as if she had said something quite awful. 'Do you mean he's an alien? I thought he was a—a half-caste of some sort, but I supposed he had a British passport.' To Jed respectability began with having a British passport.

'I told you he was from the Argentine,' Melodie reminded him, and he nodded.

'I know that, but I just thought he'd been born out there, had a foreign mother or something. I didn't realise he wasn't British. It was his name, I suppose.'

'It was his great-great-grandfather's name,' she told him. 'That's where he gets his blue eyes from too, otherwise he's as much South American as Maria Santas is.'

'You *are* in the know, aren't you?' he remarked. 'I suppose your grandfather keeps you informed?'

'Grampy knows all about it,' she agreed evasively.

'I suppose,' he guessed, 'now that the women have gone back he'll be coming over to Millway even more often.'

Melodie shrugged, non-committal. 'I suppose he might.'

'Don't you mind?'

She looked at him steadily, wondering if he would

ever come to terms with the fact that Keith and her grandfather were firm friends and nothing he said or did by way of objecting to the situation made the slightest difference.

'Grampy enjoys having him there,' she said.

'And what about you, Melly? Do you enjoy having him there?'

'I—I don't mind,' she admitted, and added hastily, 'for Grampy's sake, of course.'

It must have been her grandfather who told him, of course, Melodie realised, but she could not disguise the pleasure she felt when Keith Scott presented her with a bouquet of roses on the morning of her twenty-fourth birthday.

She opened the door in answer to his knock and took the roses from him with a cry of delight and a strange prickly feeling in her eyes. 'Happy birthday,' he said softly, and bent to kiss her before she had time to realise his intention.

She buried her face in the cool, velvety scent of the roses and knew she was blushing like a schoolgirl with pleasure. 'They're beautiful,' she said, her voice so unsteady she felt it would break. 'They're really beautiful, Keith, thank you.'

'I thought you'd be a roses girl,' he told her.

'I love any flowers at all,' she assured him, 'but roses are my favourite.'

He looked at her, his blue eyes glinting with the inevitable laughter and she hastily lowered her own. 'I thought a bouquet wouldn't be treading on any-body's toes,' he told her. 'Friend of the family and all that, nobody could object to that, could they?'

She should have frowned at the jibe against Jed,

but instead she smiled. 'You shouldn't have brought me anything at all,' she said.

'But I couldn't just let your birthday slip past without giving you *some*thing,' he objected.

'I—I suppose Grampy told you it was my birthday?' she guessed, and he nodded.

'He also told me how old you were which I admit wasn't very gentlemanly, but it *was* informative. You're not such a baby as I thought you were.'

'Oh? I thought I was pretty average for my age.'

He stood in the hall, his dark head bent over her, the blue eyes dark and glistening in the dim light. 'You're not average for any age,' he told her softly. 'You're beautiful, and no amount of discouraging frowns will make me say otherwise.'

She wasn't really frowning, only drawing her brows together in a slight crease that denoted worry rather than disapproval. If Jed too decided to make an early call on her birthday morning, it would not only be embarrassing to be found here with Keith and a huge bouquet or roses, but very difficult to explain as well.

'It's not a discouraging frown,' she confessed. 'I was—well, I was just wondering if Jed was coming over this morning too.'

'Oh, I see.' The laughter danced wickedly in his eyes. 'You're worried about being'—a black brow flicked upwards—'caught?' he suggested, and Melodie shook her head.

'No, not caught. To be caught you have to be guilty of something, and we're—I'm not.'

'Of course you're not, *amada*.' His voice was low and outrageously seductive and he bent and kissed her mouth slowly.

'Keith! Stop it!' She glanced hastily at the sitting-

169

room door, and he chuckled delightedly.

'Heaven knows what Grampy thinks I'm up to,' he said. 'Am I too early to have a word with him?'

'I wish you would,' Melodie told him feelingly. 'At least it'll give you something else to do besides plague me.'

'Do I plague you, Melodie?'

She glanced hastily at the pebble-glass front door and hid her face behind the roses. 'For heaven's sake,' she told him, 'go in and see Grampy while I let Jed in.'

Melodie had to admit to some surprise that Jed remembered her birthday or at least that he had come carrying what must be a present. He had informed her once that he considered birthday celebrations were just another commercialisation of people's sentiment. However, here he was, looking faintly sheepish and carrying a flat parcel which he handed to her almost before he was in the door.

'Many happy returns, Melly.' He gave her a chaste kiss on one cheek and seemed relieved to get the moment over.

'Oh, Jed, you remembered!' She was more touched, in fact, because he had brought her a present than because he had remembered the day, for Jed was a man who stuck firmly to his principles and he had overcome his disapproval of the idea to bring her one, because he knew it would please her.

'Of course I remembered.' He saw the bouquet then, which she had laid on the hall table while she answered the door, and he frowned. 'Roses,' he said. 'Who sent you roses, Melly?'

'Oh—oh, they're a sort of birthday present.'

'There's enough flowers there to stock a garden,' he said, thrift rearing its head. 'They must have cost a

170

fortune.'

'They're lovely, aren't they?' she said, opening her parcel and hoping to avoid naming the donor of the roses. 'I must put them in water.' She opened the paper and revealed a large shiny book, its covers appetisingly decorated with pictures of various dishes of food and the title tastefully superimposed in gold. *One Hundred Recipes from Yorkshire,* she read, and smiled as well as she was able. It was typical of Jed to be so practical and she knew he had meant it for the best, but in view of her own skill as a cook it also struck her as an odd present to buy.

'It's—it's a lovely book, Jed, thank you.'

'Mother got it for me,' he confessed. 'I'm no good at buying presents and she knows more what women like.'

'She's chosen very—very wisely.' She could not resist a brief glance at the fragrant bouquet lying on the table. 'I've been very lucky this morning.'

'Did your grandfather give you the flowers?' he asked, and Melodie hesitated before answering.

'No; Grampy gave me the most beautiful lace dress you ever saw. It's a dream, all soft and dainty and so pure white—oh, it's gorgeous, Jed. I haven't asked him yet how he came to choose it, but he has wonderful taste.'

'Lace'll not be very practical living out here,' Jed declared forthrightly, and Melodie felt as if he had slapped her. She had adored the lace dress on sight, no matter how impracticable it might be, and she had revelled in visions of herself walking into some smart restaurant and catching every eye, with the white lace complimenting her fair skin and the glossy brilliance of her hair. To be reminded that she would probably

171

never have occasion to wear it was shattering her dream rather cruelly.

'But I don't spend all my time at Millway,' she protested. 'I go out sometimes, and one day I shall——' She stopped when she saw his expression. Jed would never understand, any more than he would be likely to take her to a place where she could wear it. 'Oh well,' she said resignedly, 'I can dream, can't I?'

'Dreams don't eat anything, lass,' he told her by way of consolation, 'but there'll be more use for that book than a lace dress when you're a farmer's wife.' He frowned again when she picked up the roses from the table. 'You still haven't said who gave you the flowers,' he reminded her.

Melodie buried her face in the cool, fragrant blooms and closed her eyes in a brief ecstasy. 'Keith brought them,' she said, and went through into the kitchen before he could reply.

'Melodie!' He stood in the doorway, his round face drawn into a frown, something in his eyes that she had never seen before, but she merely flicked him a brief glance before giving her full attention to arranging the roses in a vase.

He had seldom called her Melodie before and she knew that he must be either very disturbed or very angry to have done so now. 'Will you look at me, please!' It was almost a command, and she raised her head and saw the hard glint in the hazel eyes, something quite new to her.

'I'm still listening, Jed, but I want to get my roses in water before they die.'

'I wish they *would* die!' He snatched at the bloom she held and threw it on the table with such force

172

that the head was broken and hung limply over the edge.

'Jed, don't!'

She would have gathered them up again, but he gripped her by her shoulders so tightly that his fingers dug into her, shaking her when she tried to move. 'Listen to me, Melly.'

'I am listening, but you don't have to grip me so hard, you're hurting me.'

'I'm sorry—I'm sorry.' He eased his hold on her, his first passion evidently spent, looking more familiar now, but still determined. 'I don't like Scott giving you flowers; I don't like him giving you anything. You're marrying *me*, Melly, and I object to that—that foreigner paying you attention.'

'Jed, don't be——'

'I'm not a fool, if that's what you had in mind,' he interrupted harshly. 'I have been, Melly, but not any longer. I'm going to tell Scott to leave you alone.'

'No! No, you mustn't!'

He blinked at her for a second, uncertain. 'You mean you don't *mind* him——'

'I mean I can cope with Keith Scott—or I could if there was anything to cope with in the way you suggest. He's a friend of my grandfather's, Jed, and he knew it was my birthday. What more natural thing that he should bring me a bunch of flowers as a token present? It's the sort of thing anyone would do.'

'Red roses?' he asked quietly. 'Hadn't you noticed that?'

She shook her head, although in fact it had been the first thing she noticed about her bouquet. 'They're —they're flowers, Jed, their colour doesn't mean a thing.'

'The old adage,' he declared, determined to pursue it to the bitter end. 'Red roses for love.'

'Oh, Jed, stop it! You're not making sense.'

'I don't trust him.'

'You've made that pretty obvious,' she retorted. 'What you don't seem to realise is that you're not trusting me either. If you say a word to him about—about anything, I'll never forgive you. I couldn't bear the embarrassment of having you suggest there was anything—anything like that between us.'

He was silent for a moment, evidently taking her threat seriously. 'I suppose he's here now?' he asked, and Melodie nodded. 'I thought I heard voices in the sitting-room.'

'He wanted to see Grampy and I know he's always glad to see him.'

'Which is more than can be said for me,' Jed declared.

'Oh, Jed, give him time. You're—you're so different in temperament, it isn't easy.'

'But it is with Scott.'

Melodie made a face, going back to her roses now that the worst of his temper seemed to have subsided. 'They're very much alike,' she said, 'and it doesn't make life any easier for me. Sometimes I get the feeling that they're ganging up on me.'

'Well,' Jed said firmly, 'there'll be no more of that once we're married, you'll not see Scott again, I'll see to that.'

Unable to resist the temptation any longer, Melodie tried on her dress that evening and came down in it to show her grandfather. His eyes looked at her mistily for a few moments when she came into the room, then he impatiently brushed a hand across them.

'It fits you perfectly, lass,' he told her as she walked around the room, twisting and posing in imitation of a fashion model. 'You look a real treat in it.'

She came over to him and threw her arms round his neck and kissed him. 'Oh, Grampy, it's the loveliest dress I've ever owned. The loveliest dress I'll *ever* own.' Her copper-red hair was swept up into a style that complimented the dress and she looked incredibly beautiful in the dark old room.

'It's a lovely dress, isn't it?' he agreed. 'I knew I could rely on his good taste.'

'*His* good taste?' She straightened up, her eyes wary, her hands smoothing the soft lace over her hips. 'Grampy, who got it for you?'

The old man looked at her in a way that was, uncannily, both sly and innocent. 'Why, Keith, of course. I couldn't trust anybody else to get just the right thing.'

'You mean he chose it?'

He nodded. 'All I did was give him the money and tell him I wanted you to have a dress,' he told her. 'Who else would visualise you in white lace? If I'd trusted that Jed of yours you'd probably have ended up with a raincoat and wellington boots.'

'Oh, Grampy, don't say things like that! Jed, means well, he just hasn't—well, he hasn't Keith's outlook on life, that's all.'

'I'll bet *he* didn't approve of your dress, did he?' he asked. 'I suppose you told him you'd got it?'

'Yes, of course I did.'

'*Did* he approve?'

'He—he said it wasn't very practical,' Melodie admitted.

'Did you agree with him?'

She shook her head, perching on the arm of his chair, her eyes wistful. 'I was dreaming that I was wearing it to a very expensive restaurant,' she confessed. 'Everybody turned and looked at me when I came in and I felt—felt like a famous beauty being escorted by——'

'Jed Martin?' he suggested softly, and she shook her head, relinquishing her dream yet again.

'But no matter what Jed says, I love it, Grampy, and I *will* wear it to somewhere really grand one day.'

'Is he taking you out tonight?'

'No.' She got up from the chair arm, seeking to hide the disappointment she felt. 'Jed doesn't believe in celebrating birthdays,' she told him. 'He—he thinks it's too commercialised.'

'That's one way of looking after your brass,' the old man remarked dryly, and Melodie shook her head.

'Don't, Grampy. Jed's a good man and he *does* love me in his own way, I know he does.'

The old man sighed, taking her hand in his. 'Aye, lass, I think he does, but it's a pity he couldn't have found a plain and simple girl to marry. I feel I'm sending a gazelle to a carthorse when I approve of him marrying you.'

'Grampy——' She looked up, startled by a rat-a-tat on the front door, and only realised she was still wearing the lace dress when she went to answer it.

Who she had expected to see there, she had no idea, but a serious-faced and rather dishevelled Keith was quite a surprise. He held a folded magazine in one hand and, even in the apparent haste of the moment, he spared time to appreciate the picture she made standing in the doorway.

'Melodie, can I see you for a moment?'

'Yes—yes, of course.' She stood back to admit him, wondering at the seriousness of him.

He glanced at the sitting-room door. 'It might be as well if your grandfather heard this as well,' he said.

She nodded and led the way back into the sitting-room where the old man glanced up and beamed his pleasure when he saw who the caller was. 'Come on in, lad,' he told him. 'Doesn't she look a treat in that dress?'

'Absolutely beautiful,' Keith agreed, but with much less than his usual feeling, so that Melodie and the old man looked at him curiously.

'Is something wrong, Keith?'

'Something's very wrong,' Keith told him, 'and I'm afraid I'm to blame. I should have been more careful for Melodie's sake.'

'Keith——' She looked at the magazine he held in his hand, and he thrust it at her as if he wanted to get rid of it as quickly as possible.

'Read it,' he said, 'and then you can hit me with the nearest chair and I won't blame you.'

Melodie took the magazine without a word, noting the title and today's date at the top of the page. 'County News' she read, and then a heading that implied this particular item was a social gossip column written by Joe Ennels. The name seemed to strike a note with her and she glanced up at Keith.

'The sports-writer we saw in Cydale that day,' he reminded her. 'He also writes the—the chat column in there. Read it aloud, Melodie, and then your grandfather can hear it too.'

Melodie found her heart thumping uncomfortably hard and at first words on the printed page made no sort of sense, then gradually she could recognise ones

177

that were familiar.

'—bumped into Keith Scott,' she read, 'the English-sounding, South American ex-polo-player who was once the toast of every *señorita* from his native Argentine to the lush fields of Florida and taking in Cowdray Park and other haunts of the élite. Now retired from the game, he farms several hundred acres of Yorkshire, breeding, of all things, sheep. But his taste for beautiful women seems undiminished, for his companion was a very delectable young redhead and she was wearing a ring on her third finger, left hand, so it looks as if Mr. Scott has retired from that other "sport" as well!'

The first sound Melodie heard when she stopped reading was the dry crackle of her grandfather's laugh and she looked at him reproachfully, still not quite believing the words she had just read.

'It's *not* funny, Grampy,' she chided him. 'Peter Grevill at Witten's Farm passes on his copy of *County News* to Jed. He's bound to see it.'

Keith looked at her gravely, more serious that she had ever seen him. 'I'm sorry this has happened, Melodie. I wouldn't have embarrassed you for anything, you must know that.'

'Of course she knows it,' her grandfather chimed in before she could answer for herself. 'There's one thing that you haven't thought of, though—does it strike you as at all likely that Jed Martin would read the gossip column in *any* book at all, even this one?'

'I—I suppose not,' Melodie agreed doubtfully. 'We'll just have to hope you're right, Grampy, or I don't know how I'm going to explain this time.'

CHAPTER TEN

DECIDING not to tell Jed anything about the piece in the magazine was a difficult thing to do, but Melodie thought it best in the circumstances. After all, it was just possible that he might not see it, as her grandfather had suggested, for he would have little interest in the social chatter of the area and would probably read only the more practical items that interested him.

Her grandfather and Keith had been in agreement with her decision and indeed, after his initial remorse over being the cause of a possible embarrassment to her, Keith was now back to being as self-confident and unconcerned as ever. It was still in the air whether or not Jed would see it, for she had no idea how old the magazine was when the neighbouring farmer passed it on to him.

Her grandfather had found the paragraph very amusing and she thought Keith would have done too if he had not felt a certain amount of responsibility for the effect it could have on Jed and, consequently, on her.

He was in with her grandfather now, involved in the inevitable discussion about sheep and grazing, and she was making tea for them, Mrs. Bazeley still being away. Not that Melodie minded cooking and house-work, but with such a big house and combined with her nursing duties as well, it did make life rather hectic at times.

She had just made the tea when Keith put his head

round the kitchen door and grinned when he saw how well he had timed his arrival. 'Ah,' he said, 'I thought I might be just about right for carrying the tray. What's happened to the trolley you used to use?'

'It's lost a wheel,' she told him, 'and I'm no mechanic.'

'Neither am I,' Keith admitted, 'but I'll see what I can do with it after tea if you like.' His brown face creased into a smile and his eyes teased her as she followed him from the kitchen. 'What you need,' he told her, 'is an active man around the house.'

'It would be less trouble,' Melodie retorted, 'to take a course in mechanics.'

Her grandfather, as always, was ready and waiting for his tea, but apparently he and Keith had been in the middle of some argument when Keith left to fetch the tea tray, and he was ready and eager to take it up where they had left off.

'It gives you the truth of it in that book of mine,' he said, peering at the bookshelves on the other side of the room. 'It's page—ooh, let me see, page 127, if I remember, in *The Best of English Sheep*, see if you can find it, will you, Keith? It's along that second shelf somewhere.'

'No!' Melodie was on her feet, her cheeks flushed pink when both men looked at her curiously. 'I—I'll get it,' she said, 'although why you should suddenly want that book now after all this time, Grampy, I don't know. You *never* refer to your books now.'

'Well, I am now, girl,' he informed her shortly. 'I want to show this young feller that he doesn't know all the answers yet. So don't make so much to-do about it. That's what books are for, isn't it?'

Melodie went across to the bookshelves and hesi-

180

tated before taking out the big, red-bound tome he had asked for. Her fingers trembled and she could already feel the warm flush of embarrassment in her cheeks as she anticipated the mocking laughter that would greet her when the book was opened.

'I'll—I'll take it and dust it first,' she told him, and would have managed it too, if Keith hadn't taken it from her as she passed him.

From his expression she knew that he suspected some reason for her reluctance to part with the book and his deep blue eyes sparkled mischief as he took it from her. 'Don't worry about the dust, Melodie,' he told her, his big brown hands easily breaking her grip. 'It's what's inside the pages that we're interested in, not the outside.'

'But there's——' She watched as he opened the book, unerringly, at the very place she hoped he would miss.

He stood for a second looking down at the faded, flattened tissue-paper poppies that lay between the printed pages, then he looked up at her and smiled— not the mocking smile she had expected but one that had warmth and understanding and set her heart fluttering against her ribs, reminding her of the day those poppies had been picked and secretly slipped between the pages of a book that she thought was never used.

'Megan's Folly,' he said softly, and for her ears alone, while her grandfather, as if he suspected something of what was going on, waited patiently in his chair, only his shrewd old eyes switching swiftly from one face to the other.

'They're—they're some my grandmother must have kept,' she whispered, expecting again to hear him burst into laughter at her excuse. Instead he shook his head slowly.

'They're too fresh for that,' he said. 'These are yours, *amada*.'

'I—I don't know why I kept them.' She longed to look away, but his gaze held hers inescapably. 'I—I suppose it was because—because I hadn't been there for so long.'

'Perhaps,' he agreed softly, and glanced behind her at her grandfather.

'Grampy would make too much of it,' she pleaded. 'He'd think——'

'I'm sure he would,' he told her gently, 'and who would blame him?'

'Please, Keith!'

He looked again at the fragile ghosts of the poppies, then gently closed the book on them and opened it further on. 'Here's what we're looking for,' he told the old man a moment later, and Melodie touched his hand briefly in thanks before she sat down.

'Why did you keep them, Melodie?' Keith asked. He had followed her out to the kitchen, bringing the tea-tray, and she had no need to ask to what he referred. The memory of those few minutes was too fresh in her mind. She had expected him to laugh her to scorn and instead he had smiled, as if he understood things she did not even understand herself.

'I told you,' she said, taking the things from the tray and putting them in the sink, 'I—I don't quite know why I did keep them. Now if you're going to stay out here I shall give you a drying-up cloth and put you to work.'

'Bossy!' She was elbow-deep in suds and there was

nothing she could do about the hands that slid round her waist and held her firmly, while he spoke against her ear. 'Shall I tell you why you kept those poppies?' he asked softly.

'Keith! Please don't, I'm trying to wash up, and I *know* why I kept them.'

'You said you didn't a second ago.'

'Well—well, I do.'

'So do I.'

'Will you let me go?' She squirmed ineffectively in his hold, lifting her hands from the froth of soapy bubbles when she head the door-knocker rattering loudly and urgently. 'Oh, now who can that be? Either go and answer the door or give me a towel and I'll go.'

'Bossy!' he said again, and was out of the kitchen door before she could answer.

It was only seconds before the door opened again and she turned to see Jed standing there, his face drawn into an expression so furious she could scarcely believe it was the man she knew. The already weathered cheeks were flushed a dull red, and the hazel eyes as hard and cold as glass as he stared at her from the doorway.

'Jed!'

She hastily dried her hands on a towel and turned round to face him, horribly uncertain how to react to his obvious ill-temper. Keith had evidently withdrawn and she breathed a sigh of relief for that at least.

He held a magazine in one hand and she recognised it with a sinking heart. It had been a vain hope that he would not see Joe Ennels' misleading report and in a way it was a relief to have it out in the open at last.

'I've got something here I'd like you to see,' he told

183

her in a voice so harsh and cold she would never have recognised it. He thrust the book at her. 'Read it,' he ordered, but Melodie shook her head.

'I don't have to, Jed, I've already seen it.'

'Oh, *have* you? Scott's copy, I suppose?'

Melodie nodded. 'Yes,' she said quietly, determined to hold her own temper. 'He brought it over as soon as he read it—and apologised.'

'Apologised!' His hands were clenched tight and there was nothing familiar about him at all. 'I should damned well hope he would apologise. He should do more than apologise. Do you realise half the county read this magazine? How much difficulty are they going to have in recognising you?'

'But it simply says he was with a redhead,' Melodie objected. 'I'm not the only redheaded girl in Yorkshire, Jed.'

'*I* know it's you, and that's bad enough,' Jed insisted, 'but someone else must have seen you that day *and* recognised you. Did you have to make such a fool of me, Melodie?'

'Make——' She stared at him, realising at last what was worrying him most about it. 'No one made a fool of you, Jed, and it'll die a natural death in time if you take no notice. No one takes these kind of things seriously.'

'I wouldn't know,' Jed told her. 'I don't go in for making an exhibition of myself in the papers like some men do.' He eyed her for a moment, then drew a deep breath, his mouth thin-lipped and set firm. 'It's finished as far as I'm concerned, Melodie.'

'You mean——' She stared at him unseeingly for a moment, wondering why relief was among the chaos of emotions that whirled through her mind.

'I mean Scott answering the door to me just now

184

was the last straw,' he said harshly. 'I was ready to ignore Mother's advice to finish it, when I set out I was quite ready to give you the benefit of the doubt, but seeing him——' His hands clenched tight and his face was convulsed with temper. 'He looked as if he owned the damned place; I nearly hit him!'

'There's no need for anything so silly,' she retorted. 'Keith's here to see Grampy as he always is.'

'Oh, for God's sake, Melodie, stop treating me like a complete fool!' The outburst startled her and she wouldn't have been surprised if his voice had been audible to her grandfather and Keith in the sitting-room. 'I know he didn't come from the sitting-room when he came to answer the door, although he was crafty enough to go in there after he'd let me in. He came from here—from the kitchen.'

She was determined to remain cool if she possibly could and wished now only to end the interview as quickly as she could. She looked at him steadily. 'He carried the teatray out for me,' she told him.

'Oh, you're so—so pat, aren't you?' His mouth curled into a caricature of a smile. 'Mother's right—I should have had more sense than to trust a woman with red hair. Red as a fox, sly as a fox.'

It was too much, Melodie thought wildly as she fought to control an almost hysterical laughter that welled up inside her at the trite adage. She pulled the ruby and diamond ring from her left hand and held it out to him. 'If I'm to be judged on an old wives' tale, Jed, you'd *better* have this back. There's no point to anything as long as your mother's made up her mind about me.'

'She made it up long ago,' he confirmed bluntly, and turned on his heel, the ring clutched in his hand as he

185

left the kitchen. A few seconds later she heard the front door slam, and heard her own breath release in a deep sigh.

'Melodie.' It seemed like hours since Jed had gone, but in fact a glance at her watch confirmed it was no more than half an hour. She had finished the washing up in something of a daze, not quite believing that it could have been Jed who had stormed out of the house in such a fury. His unreasonable hatred of Keith made him a different man. Or had it, she wondered, merely shown her a side of him that she had never suspected existed?

She leaned her head against the cool wall of the porch over the back door, not even turning when she heard her name. Keith came and stood close behind her, so that she was very conscious of the warmth of him and the way her hair stirred in her neck when he spoke. 'I'm sorry.'

She half turned her head and looked over her shoulder at him, finding the blue eyes disconcertingly close. 'We don't seem to be having much luck, do we?' she said. 'You with Maria and me with Jed.'

'It's finished?' She nodded, finding it surprisingly easy to accept it. 'I have a feeling I'm as much responsible for one as the other,' he told her.

She smiled wryly. 'I thought *I* was responsible for Maria going,' she said. 'At least in part.'

'Mmm, you were really,' he allowed, 'but I was the one who literally sent her packing.'

She laughed, a little wildly. 'We both seem to have a penchant for fighting our—our associations to a finish, don't we?'

'Not us,' he denied solemnly. 'Them.'

186

'Wasn't it you who lost your temper with Maria?'

'Me? Never, I don't lose my temper.'

She laughed and pulled a face at him over her shoulder. 'I've seen you in one of your more impressive rages,' she told him. 'I was very glad Maria wasn't handy when you looked like that.'

'Oh, that wasn't really a rage,' he denied blandly, one finger lifting a stray wisp of hair from her neck. 'Nothing to what Maria could produce.'

'I can imagine.'

'She accused me of being in love with you,' he told her, calmly, 'and when I agreed with her, she flew into a real rip-snorter of a rage.'

'You——' She looked up at him, her eyes wide and not quite believing.

'You've nothing against foreigners, have you?' he asked, and his hands turned her round until she was held close against him, and had to tip back her head to look at him.

'Not really,' she allowed, trying to keep her voice steady and sound as matter-of-fact about it as he did when all the time she could feel the dizzying thud of her heart and knew she was all shiny-eyed and blushing like a schoolgirl. 'But I've no intention of joining a harem,' she warned him.

The blue eyes looked down at her and he laughed, the sound that always sent a chilling trickle of excitement down her spine and curled her toes. 'I've retired, remember?' he said. 'The man in the paper said so.'

'Keith.' She hesitated, realising how different it always was with Keith in the position that Jed should have been and never was. He had never held her like Keith did, never kissed her as Keith had, and she had been in love with him far longer than she had realised.

'I love you,' she told him at last, and looked at him as if she was, in a way, seeing him for the first time.

'I've loved you, *amada*, ever since you ordered me off Grampy's land for the first time.'

'Grampy!' She looked at him wide-eyed. 'What's he going to say?'

'Something like—I told you so, I imagine,' he informed her calmly. 'When I left him just now he told me that if you hadn't promised to marry me by the time he was ready for his dinner, I wasn't half the man he thought I was.'

'You mean—you and he——' She pouted her lips in disapproval. 'You two are always ganging up on me,' she complained, 'and I——'

'Will you be quiet?' Keith told her sternly. 'How can I kiss you when you're talking? Unless,' he added a few minutes later, 'you're ready to say you'll marry me?'

It was never actually said, but through a rather rosy haze, it crossed Melodie's mind that the kitchen was not the most romantic place to propose.

A Treasury of Harlequin Romances!

Many of the all time favorite Harlequin Romance Novels have not been available, until now, since the original printing. But on this special introductory offer, they are yours in an exquisitely bound, rich gold hardcover with royal blue imprint. Three complete unabridged novels in each volume. And the cost is so very low you'll be amazed!

This very special collection of classic Harlequin Romances would be a distinctive addition to your library. And imagine what a delightful gift they'd make for any Harlequin reader!

Start your collection now. See reverse of this page for **SPECIAL INTRODUCTORY OFFER!**

v

FREE!

Harlequin
Romance
Catalogue

Here is a wonderful opportunity to read many of the Harlequin Romances you may have missed.

The HARLEQUIN ROMANCE CATALOGUE lists hundreds of titles which possibly are no longer available at your local bookseller. To receive your copy, just fill out the coupon below, mail it to us, and we'll rush your catalogue to you!

Following this page you'll find a sampling of a few of the Harlequin Romances listed in the catalogue. Should you wish to order any of these immediately, kindly check the titles desired and mail with coupon.

To: **HARLEQUIN READER SERVICE, Dept. N 305**
     M.P.O. Box 707, Niagara Falls, N.Y. 14302
     Canadian address: Stratford, Ont., Canada

☐ Please send me the free Harlequin Romance Catalogue.

☐ Please send me the titles checked.

    I enclose $_____ (No C.O.D.'s), All books are 60c each. To help defray postage and handling cost, please add 25c.

Name _____

Address _____

City/Town _____

State/Prov. _____ Zip_____

Have You Missed Any of These

Harlequin Romances?

☐ 446 TO PLEASE THE DOCTOR
Marjorie Moore

☐ 454 NURSE IN LOVE
Jane Arbor

☐ 467 NURSE TO THE ISLAND
Caroline Trench

☐ 974 NIGHT OF THE HURRICANE
Andrea Blake

☐ 980 A SONG BEGINS
Mary Burchell

☐ 992 SNARE THE WILD HEART
Elizabeth Hoy

☐ 999 GREENFINGERS FARM
Joyce Dingwell

☐ 1132 DARK HORSE, DARK RIDER
Elizabeth Hoy

☐ 1150 THE BRIDE OF MINGALAY
Jean S. Macleod

☐ 1255 LITTLE SAVAGE
Margaret Malcolm

☐ 1269 PRETENCE
Roberta Leigh

☐ 1302 TEACHERS MUST LEARN
Nerina Hilliard

☐ 1309 THE HILLS OF MAKETU
Gloria Bevan

☐ 1323 MOONLIGHT ON THE WATER
Hilda Nickson

☐ 1340 THE HOUSE OF YESTERDAY
Margaret Malcolm

☐ 1342 THE FEEL OF SILK
Joyce Dingwell

☐ 1343 TAMBOTI MOON
Wynne May

☐ 1345 THREE NURSES
Louise Ellis

☐ 1347 THE TRUANT SPIRIT
Sara Seale

☐ 1348 REVOLT AND VIRGINIA
Essie Summers

☐ 1349 ETERNAL SUMMER
Anne Hampson

☐ 1350 ABOVE RUBIES
Mary Cummins

☐ 1354 WHEN LOVE'S BEGINNING
Mary Burchell

☐ 1355 RISING STAR
Kaye Thorpe

☐ 1358 HOME TO WHITE WINGS
Jean Dunbar

☐ 1359 RETURN TO TREMARTH
Susan Barrie

☐ 1363 STAR DUST
Margaret Malcolm

☐ 1364 ONE LOVE
Jean S. Macleod

☐ 1365 HOTEL SOUTHERLY
Joyce Dingwell

☐ 1366 DESIGN FOR LOVING
Margaret Baumann

☐ 1368 MUSIC I HEARD WITH YOU
Elizabeth Hoy

☐ 1370 THE WAYS OF LOVE
Catherine Airlie

☐ 1371 DANCING ON MY HEART
Belinda Dell

☐ 1372 ISLE OF POMEGRANATES
Iris Danbury

☐ 1373 THE PIED TULIP
Elizabeth Ashton

☐ 1375 THE KINDLED FIRE
Essie Summers

☐ 1377 SISTER DARLING
Marjorie Norrell

☐ 1378 NURSE SMITH, COOK
Joyce Dingwell

☐ 1379 A TOUCH OF STARLIGHT
Rosemary Pollock

☐ 1384 BELOVED ENEMIES
Pamela Kent

☐ 1387 THE HOUSE CALLED GREEN
BAYS, Jan Andersen

☐ 1398 FEAST OF THE CANDLES
Iris Danbury

☐ 1400 THE DISTANT TRAP
Gloria Bevan

☐ 1405 THE CURTAIN RISES
Mary Burchell

☐ 1406 WALK INTO THE WIND
Jane Arbor

☐ 1407 NEXT STOP GRETNA
Belinda Dell

☐ 1414 SOWN IN THE WIND
Jean S. Macleod

☐ 1419 SO ENCHANTING AN ENEMY
Margaret Malcolm

All books are 60c. Please use the handy order coupon.

AA